Avoch School 1969/70

PRIZE

awarded to

Anita MacIver

for

Needlework

Secondary 2

R Reid

THE CLUE IN THE
CRUMBLING WALL

TITLES IN THE SERIES

Nancy Drew Mystery Stories

THE CLUE IN THE
CRUMBLING WALL

BY

CAROLYN KEENE

(*A Sampson Low Book*)

MACDONALD
LONDON

CONTENTS

Chapter I

STRANGERS IN THE GARDEN

GREAT drops of rain pelted the sidewalk, as Nancy Drew raced madly toward home, her golden hair flying in the stiff breeze.

"This is going to be a bad storm," the girl thought, glancing up anxiously at the boiling black clouds.

All along the residential street, people were running to shelter. Doors and windows were being closed hastily.

The summer day had been unusually sultry, but now the air was chilly. The wind blew in strong gusts, whipping the trees and bushes wildly. A large branch from a maple crashed down directly in front of Nancy. A woman on a porch saw the girl and called to her anxiously.

"Won't you wait here until the storm is over?"

"Oh, thank you, I'll make it all right," Nancy said in reply, and hurried on.

She took a short cut through a neighbour's driveway, arriving breathless at her own home just as a jagged streak of lightning cut the sky behind her. It was followed by a deafening crash of thunder. Hannah Gruen, the Drews' middle-aged housekeeper, met Nancy at the door.

"Thank goodness, you're home safe!" she cried in relief.

The kindly woman cared for the motherless girl as lovingly as if she were her own daughter, and worried a great deal whenever she thought harm might befall her.

The rain, which lasted for twenty minutes, came down in such torrents that for a time everything was blotted from view. When it ended, Nancy gazed ruefully from a window at her garden. She was dismayed to see the tall hollyhocks snapped off near the ground. Clumps of painted daisies were flattened in the mud.

"My lovely garden is a wreck," she said to Mrs. Gruen, "and—why, my goodness!"

The girl dashed out of doors. The housekeeper followed, wanting to know what the trouble was. Nancy stared in consternation at the flower border.

"My beautiful new rose bushes!" she gasped. "They're gone!"

Where four choice bushes had been planted only the week before, there now appeared four gaping holes filled with water.

"I suppose the wind——" began Mrs. Gruen.

"I'm sure it wasn't the wind, because the bushes would be around somewhere, and they're not," Nancy objected, already searching the garden. "I planted them very deep, anyway. I'm afraid they've been stolen!"

"But who would take them?" asked the housekeeper.

"I don't know, but good rose bushes are scarce this year and ours were rare specimens."

"The police should be notified," Hannah Gruen said with determination, and went into the house to telephone to them.

Nancy continued to gaze about the garden. Except for the rose bushes, no other shrubs or plants were missing. It was very mystifying, and even more so when Mrs. Gruen appeared to say that the same kind of loss had been reported by other people. An investigator would be sent to the Drew home to make an inspection.

"There's no question but that your rose bushes were stolen, Nancy," the woman added grimly.

"And I'm afraid they won't be recovered," sighed Nancy.

"Unless you should decide to search for them yourself," Hannah Gruen said with a twinkle in her eye. "As a detective, I'd certainly favour you over anyone on the River Heights police force!"

Nancy smiled at the compliment. Modest and unassuming, she never would admit she possessed any particular talents. Nearly everyone in River Heights, however, knew that the girl was as clever as she was pretty. Over a span of a few years she had solved many baffling mysteries.

As Nancy and the housekeeper busied themselves gathering up debris from the garden, they heard the familiar song of one of River Heights' well-known characters.

"Here comes old Mehearty down the street!" Nancy laughed, shaking off her sombre mood. "Do you want any clams today?"

"I do not," Mrs. Gruen said with emphasis. "But if I know Mehearty, he'll probably talk me into buying some anyway!"

The old man, once a sailor, had received his nickname from Nancy when she was a little girl. He often addressed other people as "me hearties," and sang nautical songs including these words. Little Nancy had gotten the whole thing mixed up and called him "Mehearty man." Her nickname had stuck to him. Mehearty was a good-natured, lovable person, full of yarns of the sea. An injury on shipboard had kept him on land for many years. He dug clams in the near-by river and sold them for a living.

The man's cart bell tinkled merrily, and a moment later the jolly, weather-beaten old fellow rounded the corner of the driveway, wheeling his little wagon. Spying Nancy and the housekeeper, he began to carol:

"Clams by the bushel,
Clams by the lot,
Clams for the kettle,
Clams for the pot."

"None for us today," Mrs. Gruen called, starting toward the house.

Old Mehearty smiled his most winning smile. "Real cheap today," he coaxed. "Ye can't turn down my clams, me hearties. Why, my clams are nutritious, my clams are delicious, my clams are delectable, my clams are respectable!"

Nancy laughed, but Mrs. Gruen said seriously, "I'm in no

mood to buy clams, respectable or otherwise right now! We've just discovered that four of our best rose bushes have been stolen."

"Ye don't say!" The old man's blue eyes roved to the gaping holes in the flower border. "Now that's what I call bad luck, ma'am, but ye can turn it into good luck if ye've a mind to."

"How, may I ask?"

"By buyin' Mehearty's good Muskoka River clams!"

"And in what way would that help?"

"Why, ye might find a pearl in one of 'em," the old fellow chuckled. "Then ye could use the money to buy a dozen rose bushes!"

"Did anyone ever find a pearl in one of your clams?" Nancy inquired curiously.

"Just ask Jasper Hawkins on Pinewood Point!" the old man boasted. "'Tweren't a very big pearl nor a very valuable one, but a pearl just the same. Jasper sold it, too."

"Upon second thought," remarked Mrs. Gruen, "I believe I could use a dozen or two of your clams, Mehearty. Nancy, please run into the house for my purse."

The girl darted away, returning with the pocketbook and a container for the clams. After the old sailor had gone on down the street singing about his wares, she and Hannah bore their purchase into the spic and span kitchen.

"I wish we could find a pearl," Nancy remarked, smiling. "What I couldn't do with a little extra cash right now!"

"Then suppose you help me open the clams," the housekeeper suggested, handing the girl a sharp knife. "Maybe you'll find a pearl. I've heard that somebody in River Heights once found a large one in a Muskoka River clam."

"Then there's a chance for me," said Nancy, starting her work with gusto.

"Have a care or you'll slash off a finger! that knife is sharp," Hannah Gruen advised.

Nancy nodded and paid close attention to her task. Soon she had a pile of empty clam shells, but no pearl.

"Bother!" she exclaimed impatiently. "I don't believe Mehearty's clams ever have anything in them but meat! I'm glad this is the last one!"

Cutting it open, Nancy glanced carelessly inside. As she was about to toss away the shells, a tiny object on one of them drew her attention. Scarcely daring to hope what it might be, she examined the shell. Embedded in it was a small white object!

"I *have* found a pearl!" she cried, holding it out for the housekeeper to see.

The woman stared at the pearl. "I declare it *is* one," she acknowledged, "and it may be worth money!"

"I'll take it downtown to old Mr. Weatherby and ask him," said Nancy eagerly.

Sam Weatherby was a dealer in curios and odd jewellery. Bubbling over with excitement, the girl removed the pearl, washed it, and took it to the old man's shop. Once there, she was annoyed to have to wait fifteen minutes while an unpleasant man bargained with the shop owner over the price of an antique watch charm he hoped to sell. At last the customer pocketed some money and turned on his heel, remarking:

"I might as well have given it to you!"

"That was Hector Keep, the lawyer," Mr. Weatherby remarked to Nancy after the man had left. "How he loves to argue! If all my customers were like him, I'd have to close up shop. Well, what can I do for you, Miss Drew?"

Removing the pearl from her purse, Nancy asked the curio dealer for an estimate of its value.

"Well, well," the man said, examining the object carefully. "Pretty nice. It's worth a fair sum. Where'd you get this?"

"From a Muskoka River clam."

A look of astonishment spread over the man's face. In a few moments he mumbled:

"I once bought a river pearl from Jasper Hawkins, but I never expected to see another one so good."

"You'll buy mine?" Nancy asked eagerly.

"I will, and pay you a good price, too, if you'll bring me the shells from which it was taken. I want to display the pearl with them." The dealer smiled. "I suppose now we'll have a rush of folks diggin' clams!"

Nancy replaced the pearl in her pocketbook and hastened from the shop to get the desired shells. So intent was she upon her good fortune that she failed to observe a strange-looking young man who had been standing outside the shop, and who now followed only a few paces behind her. Unaware of impending trouble, Nancy carried her purse lightly under her arm.

Presently she passed a department store on a street thronged with shoppers and gazed into the windows. The man drew closer to Nancy. Then, so suddenly that she scarcely knew what happened, he jerked the purse from beneath her arm and fled!

Chapter II

HEATH CASTLE

IT took Nancy a moment to recover from her astonishment. By the time she whirled around, the purse snatcher already was running down the street. The girl dashed after him, trying to avoid bumping into pedestrians.

"What's the matter?" asked a man she sidestepped just in time.

"My purse——"

He took up the chase with her. As word spread, other people followed. But the thief was fleet-footed. Nancy caught a faint glimpse of him as he dashed into an alley and over a fence, but not enough of a glimpse to identify him. She did note that he was very young, and that he wore ill-fitting, bulky clothes.

Nancy stopped. "Not a chance to overtake him now," she

said unhappily. Then she added, "Well, there goes my pearl!"

Besides the pearl, her purse had contained a vanity case, a lovely lace handkerchief, and about seventy cents in change.

"I suppose I should be thankful I didn't lose more," the girl decided ruefully, as she thanked the strangers who had tried to assist her.

Nancy walked on down the street. The Central police station was located at the next intersection, and on impulse she stopped in to report her loss.

"We'll do what we can to help you," the desk sergeant assured her, writing down the information after he had heard her story. "Two thefts in an hour from one person. That's quite a record!"

Nancy left the place without much conviction that the stolen purse would be recovered more readily than the rose bushes. Arriving home a few minutes later, she was surprised to find a young policewoman in uniform talking earnestly to Hannah Gruen.

"Nancy, this is Lieutenant Masters," the housekeeper introduced her. "She was sent to investigate the theft of our rose bushes, and has mentioned several facts that will interest you."

Lieutenant Masters was a charming woman; not the least masculine despite her businesslike manner. She had been placed in charge of juvenile delinquency in River Heights only a short time ago, and already was having much success in her work.

"Our Chief speaks very highly of you, Miss Drew," she complimented Nancy in a rich, cultured voice. "Also of your distinguished father. Your last case, I believe, concerned *The Secret in the Old Attic*."

"Grandfather March's," supplied Nancy, smiling faintly. "It was fun solving the mystery of that queer old place, but I'm afraid the newspapers overplayed my part."

"I'm sure they didn't," replied the policewoman, smiling. "Isn't it true that you've been interested in mysteries ever since you were a little girl?"

"I can't seem to resist them," Nancy admitted. "They fascinate me."

"Her father encourages her," spoke up Mrs. Gruen. "Mr. Drew, you know, is a lawyer, and now and then he has a mystery he turns over to her to solve. One of her first cases was written up in the newspapers as The Bungalow Mystery. Since then I've lost count of them."

"I haven't solved them alone," Nancy said quickly. "My friends, Bess Marvin and George Fayne, helped me." She added that George was a girl, and a very active one at that.

"At any rate, the Chief gives you credit for real talent," the woman smiled. "Now for the case at hand. You have no idea who may have run off with your rose bushes?"

"Not the slightest."

"I may have a clue. They probably were taken by an eight-year-old child."

"By a child!" Nancy exclaimed.

"Yes, the case is a strange one with mysterious angles."

"Please tell me about it. I can't see why a child would want those rose bushes."

"The girl in question has a passionate love for flowers and an amazing knowledge of them. In recent weeks she has taken seeds, plants, and even shrubs to satisfy her longing."

"I've already told Lieutenant Masters that we'll not prefer charges against a child," Hannah Gruen explained to Nancy. "I feel that her parents are more to blame than she is."

"Joan's father is not living," the young officer resumed. "Her widowed mother is ill and very poor."

"Then please forget that we ever made a report of the affair," Nancy requested.

"No. I'll see that the bushes are returned to your garden. It is best that Joan do that. Mrs. Fenimore will insist upon it, anyway, for she is greatly distressed by her child's strange behaviour."

"There must be a reason for such queer actions," commented Mrs. Gruen.

"There is," nodded the policewoman. "If I had more time, I'd probe the mystery of the Fenimores."

"Mystery?" questioned Nancy alertly.

"I'm on my way to their house now," Lieutenant Masters smiled, pleased to note Nancy's interest. "Why not come with me? Then you can hear everything first-hand."

"I'd love to go."

Nancy rode with the young woman to the Fenimore cottage which was located in a poor section of the city and which was greatly in need of repair. The tiny yard was a mass of flowers, however, and vines considerably half-covered the unpainted, tumbledown porch.

As Nancy and the officer went up the flagstone walk, the policewoman called attention to four rose bushes newly planted beside the sagging porch.

"Are these yours?" she asked.

"They look like the ones we lost," Nancy admitted. "But, please, I don't want to get a child into trouble——"

She broke off, because a little girl in a faded pink dress had just come around a corner of the house. Seeing the woman in uniform, she stopped short and then turned as if to run off.

"Don't be afraid," the lieutenant said kindly.

"Did you come to take me away?" the little girl asked.

"Indeed we didn't, Joan. But I'm afraid we'll have to send you off to a special school unless you decide to be good."

"I am good," Joan said, tossing her blonde, tangled curls. "Just ask my mother!"

"In many ways you are very good. I know you work hard and you take care of your mother. But why do you dig up shrubs and plants that don't belong to you?"

Joan's gaze roved to the telltale rose bushes. She hung her head and did not answer.

"I'm sure you don't really mean to be naughty," went on the policewoman. "Why do you take flowers?"

"Because they're pretty," Joan said with a trace of defiance. "We can never buy anything nice."

Sinking down on the porch steps, the child began to cry. The young policewoman comforted her. Soon she gained an admission from the little girl that an older boy, Jeddy Hooker, who lived next door, had suggested that Joan help herself to the rose bushes.

"I don't know why I did it," the little girl sobbed. "I wish my Aunt Florianna would come home. Then we could have nice things."

In an undertone, Lieutenant Masters explained to Nancy that Aunt Florianna, whose real name was Flossie Johnson, had been missing many years. The woman, a talented dancer, had disappeared while on a vacation trip.

"Joan only knows about her aunt from her mother," the lieutenant added. "Mrs. Fenimore wasn't married when her sister disappeared. Since Mr. Fenimore's death she has been ill and has had very little money. It's too bad Florianna can't be found, so she might help her."

"It's a shame," said Nancy soberly. "Did she run away deliberately?"

"Come inside and let Mrs. Fenimore tell you the story herself," the policewoman suggested.

Nancy received a distinct shock as Joan led the callers into the living room of the house. Lying on a faded couch was a sweet-faced woman with deep lines of suffering on her forehead. The Drew girl was sure Mrs. Fenimore was not more than thirty years old, yet she looked fifty.

"I'm glad to meet you, Miss Drew," she said in a soft voice. "Please pardon such an ungracious way of receiving you, but my illness——"

"I'm sorry you're not feeling well," Nancy replied. "Perhaps it would be better if I came some other time."

"No, no."

"If you feel strong enough, Mrs. Fenimore," said Lieutenant Masters, "I wish you would tell Miss Drew about your sister's disappearance. She was asking me whether you think Florianna dropped out of sight deliberately."

"I can't believe it of Flossie—that's what I always call her. She took the name of Florianna when she became a dancer,"

exclaimed the woman. "She went away for a month's rest
and never was heard of again."

"If Aunt Florianna would come home, we'd live in a
castle," Joan blurted out. "We'd have beautiful gardens and
everything nice. Aunt Florianna would be rich."

At Nancy's look of surprise, Mrs. Fenimore explained that
the dancer had been engaged to a wealthy manufacturer
named Walter Heath. Five years after her strange disappearance he had died, leaving Heath Castle and the rest
of his estate to her.

"There is a provision in the will which keeps me from
collecting my sister's inheritance," said Mrs. Fenimore. "You
see, Mr. Heath tied up the property by stipulating that if
Florianna did not return to claim the estate within five
years, the grounds were to be converted into a county park."

"Where is the property located?" asked Nancy.

"Several miles up the Muskoka River. The place is called
Heath Castle. Once it was a very beautiful estate with
walled gardens and sunken pools. Now I'm told it looks
more like a jungle."

"Legally the property still belongs to Florianna?" Nancy
inquired.

"It does for the next three weeks. After that she loses all
claim to it. Oh, I do wish for Joan's sake my sister would
come back."

"Mr. Heath tried to trace Florianna before his death,"
Lieutenant Masters revealed. "But the detectives he engaged
failed to turn up a single clue."

The story deeply interested Nancy. She shrewdly guessed
that the policewoman had hoped to intrigue her with details
of the case. Confirming this suspicion, the young woman
officer suggested that the girl might find it worth her while
to visit Heath Castle soon.

Before they left the cottage, Nancy and Miss Masters
helped Joan prepare some supper. Wishing to spare Mrs.
Fenimore any embarrassment, they refrained from discuss-
ing Joan's latest escapade.

The circumstances which had caused the petty theft continued to trouble Nancy, however. That night at dinner she told the story to the housekeeper, regretting that her father was not at home to hear it. The following day she repeated it to her friends, Bess Marvin and George Fayne. The two girls, who were cousins, were particularly interested in the part dealing with Heath Castle.

"What are we waiting for?" George cried enthusiastically. "Why not go there right away and explore the place?"

"Will it be safe?" asked Bess cautiously.

"It won't be an easy trip," Nancy warned her friends. "The estate is several miles from here and I'm told the undergrowth is like a jungle. The best way to get there is by motorboat up the Muskoka River."

Twenty minutes later the three girls rented a small motorboat at Campbell's Landing. The old craft leaked a bit and the engine clattered and threw oil.

"Lucky we all know how to swim," Bess said with some misgiving, as they pulled away from the dock. "I have a feeling this old tub may sink before we go very far."

"We'll be all right if George does her stuff with the bailer!" Nancy laughed, heading the craft upstream.

The river was wide near town, but the upper reaches were narrow and twisted and turned at such sharp angles that fast travel was out of the question. At the steering wheel, Nancy kept an alert watch for stumps and shoals.

"It's really pretty along here, but so wild," Bess commented, her gaze wandering along the solid line of trees fringing the shores.

"Better forget the scenery for a while," Nancy advised, "and give George a hand with the bailing. If you don't, our shoes will be soaked."

At the bow of the boat water was slowly seeping in. Both Bess and George fell to work, vigorously dipping it out. They became so absorbed in what they were doing that they no longer watched the shore.

"Listen!" Nancy presently said. "What was that?"

Bess and George had heard no unusual sound, but they stood up to look around.

"A motorboat!" Nancy exclaimed. "Oh, now you can hear the engine plainly. But where is it?"

As she spoke, a small blue and white painted craft shot out from one of the river's many hidden tributaries. Until that moment it had been screened from view by overhanging bushes.

"Look out!" Bess cried in alarm.

The man in the oncoming boat had not seen the girls. At high speed he raced straight toward their little craft.

Desperately Nancy spun the wheel. There was not enough space to clear.

With a splintering crash, the two boats collided!

Chapter III

A RUNAWAY BOAT

THE speeding boat which had struck Nancy's craft veered sharply away and raced downstream.

"Hey, wait!" George shouted angrily at the reckless pilot. "You've damaged our boat! Nancy, go after him! Don't let him get away!"

Nancy, however, was busy with another problem. When the crash had come, she had seen Bess lose her balance, strike her head on the side of the boat, and topple into the water.

If Bess were unconscious, there was no time to lose! Nancy instantly turned off the motor, located the spot where her friend had gone down, and dived in. Grasping the stunned girl under the shoulders with her left arm, she struck out with the other for the boat. George leaned over and helped pull the unconscious victim aboard.

"Is she——?" her cousin began in a terrified voice.

At this moment Bess opened her eyes and coughed several times. Nancy thumped her on the back.

"I'm—all—right," Bess said weakly. "Our boat——" She tried to point.

For the first time the others realized that water was filling the craft at an alarming rate from a small hole in its side.

"Quick, George! Bail!" shouted Nancy.

George picked up the can she had been using before, and started to work. Nancy leaped forward, crumpled up a newspaper lying on the bottom of the boat, and stuffed it into the hole. Looking in a tackle box near her, she discovered a burlap sack, which she rolled up and added to the paper. In a moment the influx of rushing water was stayed.

"Good!" panted George, sitting down. "Now we can chase that other boat!"

It was not in sight, however, and Nancy wisely decided it would be useless to try to pursue the speedier craft. She turned her attention to Bess.

"How are you feeling?" she asked.

"Oh, all right, I guess, but—but I'd like to go home."

"We'll go right away," decided Nancy. "I'm a sight myself, and this boat can't stand much more."

"I wish we hadn't lost the fellow who ruined it," said George. "If I ever see him——" she added angrily.

"Would you recognize him?" asked Nancy.

George confessed that she would not, and inquired if the other girls would. Bess had not noticed him, but Nancy replied:

"I didn't see him very well. But I believe I'd know him if we ever meet again. At any rate, I'm going to keep my eyes open for both him and his boat."

The girls dreaded to return to Campbell's Landing with their damaged craft. But the owner was not disagreeable about the matter.

"It won't cost more than ten dollars to repair it," he assured them. "I'll do the work myself." Nancy promised to pay him, and he added, "You'd better hunt for that scoundrel who hit you, and make him give you the money. He ain't got no right runnin' into folks thataway."

Discouraged that the trip to Heath Castle had been a

failure, Nancy took her friends home, then went to her own house. The following day found her still without a clue to the identity of the unknown boatman. Though she described his blue and white craft to several persons, no one was able to identify it. Then suddenly she thought of someone who might.

"Old Mehearty," she told Hannah Gruen. "I believe I'll hike down to his place on the river and chat with him."

Taking Bess along for company, she proceeded toward the river. As the girls approached the docks, they observed a dark-haired, beady-eyed stranger coming up the boardwalk. Instantly Nancy was struck by his resemblance to the man who had crashed into her boat. She stopped to speak to him, inquiring if he were not the one who had caused the collision.

"No, I'm not!" the man snapped. "I don't even own a boat!" Glaring at the girls, he walked on hurriedly.

The unpleasant encounter disheartened Nancy and she was silent until they reached Mehearty's little home. Then her spirits revived. The place was very quaint. Once it had been a small, well-appointed yacht. Now it was a beached wreck, weathered by sun and rain. Its only claim to any former glory was the flag which flew proudly from the afterdeck.

"Anyone home?" Nancy called, cupping her hands.

"Come in, come in!" invited the old sailor in a loud voice.

He was sitting inside the cabin with his feet on a built-in table, eating a lunch of baked beans out of a tin can, and some tomatoes. Seeing the girls, he got to his feet, greatly pleased to receive their call.

"Ye honour me, comin' here," he said, his blue eyes twinkling. "But I'm goin' to have to disappoint ye. I've nary a clam today. Too lazy to go out and dig 'em, I guess."

"Oh, we didn't come to buy clams," Nancy replied, glancing curiously about the inside of the yacht which she had never seen before.

The room was small and cluttered, but very clean. Mehearty's bunk was neatly made, and on a shelf above it was displayed an amazing array of sea shells.

"I collect 'em," the sailor explained, following Nancy's gaze. "Some o' those shells came from Puget Sound and some from the South Pacific." Hobbling over to the shelf, he pointed to a curious-looking specimen. "That's called the washboard clam. It's one of the biggest of our river clams."

"How interesting!" the girls exclaimed.

Pleased by their attention, the man showed them other shells which were too large to stand on the shelf. One, measuring three feet across, had come from an island in the Pacific.

"My, think what a pearl one might find in a clam that size!" Nancy laughed, then told of her own loss, saying she was glad the pearl was not large. "Mehearty, what would you say is the largest one ever discovered?"

"Well, now that's a poser. The largest pearl I ever heard tell of weighed about three ounces. There's probably bigger ones yet to be found."

"That's amazing!" said Bess.

The old sailor showed the girls other treasures from the sea: huge, fluted specimens and tiny, delicate shells from the Orient. Amazed at the variety in his collection, Nancy asked Mehearty if he had obtained the many different kinds by going to the various places where they could be found.

"No," the clam digger laughed. "Mr. Heath gave 'em to me."

The name startled Nancy.

"Not Walter Heath?" she inquired alertly.

"No. Ira Heath—Walt's father," Mehearty answered. "He gave me the shells when he had his button factory on the inlet."

"A button factory near here?" Bess asked in surprise. "That's news to me."

"The factory's been closed for years. It was shut down when the supply of fresh water mussels gave out. They use 'em, you know, to make buttons."

Nancy and Bess were learning a great deal, and they wanted to learn more.

"What became of Mr. Heath?" Nancy inquired.

"Ira was born in England and went back there on a visit," Mehearty revealed, lighting a corn cob pipe. "He died there. His son Walt was left in charge here, and he stayed on at Heath Castle."

"His father built the castle?" inquired Bess.

Mehearty nodded, warming to the story. "Yes, Heath Castle was built to look like one o' them fancy English places. The gardens were wonderful—a sight to set your eyes ablaze! Stone walls everywhere, with flowers and vines, and all kinds o' trees from everywhere in the world."

Nancy was becoming more eager every minute to see the estate.

"But for me," went on the clam digger, "the place is too lonesome. No houses close by. The old gent built it 'bout a mile up the river from the button factory. Since Walt died 'bout five years ago, no one ever goes near the castle, or near the factory on Harper's Inlet, either."

"Harper's Inlet?" Nancy repeated thoughtfully. "Someone must have been there yesterday."

"That's right," agreed Bess. "We saw a motorboat come out of the inlet. It crashed into our boat and threw me into the water."

"Queer," commented Mehearty. "I don't know what business anyone would have at the factory. Who was the fellow?"

"That's what we came to find out," Nancy said.

She gave a complete account of the accident. Mehearty could not identify the man from her description, but he promised to watch for such a person.

"I'll keep an eye out for that boat, too," he added thoughtfully. "Can't figure why the fellow would be prowling up the inlet. Fishin's no good there. Maybe I'll run up and have a look."

Satisfied that Mehearty would be able to locate the boat and its mysterious pilot if anyone could, Nancy and Bess thanked him and left his quaint yacht home.

"How about going to Heath Castle now?" Nancy suggested to her friend.

"Sorry," Bess replied, "but I can't go today. Let's do it tomorrow. Then maybe George can go with us."

Nancy agreed, and the girls separated. When she reached home, a surprise awaited her. While she and Mrs. Gruen had been away from the house, four rose bushes had been planted in the garden. Examination disclosed that they were the same ones that had been taken, and were only slightly wilted from having been moved twice.

"Joan must have brought them back!" Nancy declared. "Oh, I'm so glad, for I'm sure she wouldn't have taken them if that boy Jeddy Hooker hadn't urged her to."

She was pressing dirt firmly about the bushes when her father drove into the garage. The girl stopped her work at once and ran to greet him. Mr. Drew was a distinguished-looking man, tall and handsome.

"Hello, Nancy," he smiled fondly. "How's the garden?"

"Rather successful today," she laughed. "Four rose bushes that were taken yesterday are home again. I wish all mysteries could be solved as easily."

As they went into the house together, Nancy told him about the boat accident, the Fenimore problems, and the mystery of Florianna.

"Dad, tell me all you can about Ira Heath and his son Walter," she asked. "Did you know them?"

"Only by reputation. For years they operated a very successful button factory. Then the business went to pieces."

"I already know that part," Nancy said. "What about Heath Castle? After Ira and Walter died, who took charge of the place?"

"Hector Keep, I believe."

Nancy's mind flew to the unpleasant customer in the curio dealer's shop.

"Isn't he a lawyer?" she asked.

"Yes," Mr. Drew agreed soberly, "but I'll confess that Keep's brand of law never appealed to me. I consider him a shrewd, calculating man."

"Is there any reason why he should allow Heath Castle to go to ruin?"

"None that I know of."

"Do you think Mr. Keep did everything to find Florianna?" Nancy asked thoughtfully.

"So far as I know, he did. I can't see any reason why he shouldn't have."

"Did you know her?"

"I saw her perform many times. I admired her dancing very much," Mr. Drew replied, smiling in reminiscence. "Why she should have disappeared at the height of her career has always puzzled me."

"Apparently she left no clues behind," remarked Nancy.

"The case was a strange one," her father said. "I guess Walter Heath was pretty broken up over it. I've always wondered——"

"You've wondered what, Dad?"

"Well, it occurred to me that Heath Castle might provide a key to the mystery. I've no real reason for thinking so—it's merely a hunch I have."

"And I have a similar one!" Nancy cried jubilantly. "Two Drew minds can't be wrong!" she laughed. "Tomorrow I'll go there and ask those crumbling old walls to give up their secret!"

Chapter IV

THE HAUNTED WALK

THE following morning found Nancy, Bess, and George motoring to Heath Castle. By studying a map of the district, they had discovered a little-used road which led to the abandoned estate. Though this woodland route was rough and dusty, Bess preferred it to another boat trip.

"Hope we don't ruin a tyre," Nancy remarked, manoeuvring the car to avoid sharp rocks. "How much farther to Heath Castle?"

George peered at the speedometer, noting that they had travelled more than five miles from the outskirts of River Heights.

"We're coming to something!" she cried a moment later.

Through the trees, the girls caught a fleeting glimpse of a sharply pitched, rust-coloured roof. The car rounded a sharp curve, blotting it from view. Then the road ended abruptly in front of a high, vine-covered stone wall.

"The boundaries of the estate!" Bess announced. "Yes, there's the name *Heath Castle* on the iron gate!"

"And the gate is locked—fastened with a chain," Nancy observed, turning off the engine.

"How do we get in?" asked Bess.

"Over the top, Commando style," laughed George. In her eagerness, she tripped as she sprang from the automobile.

Nancy and Bess, following their chum, gazed with misgiving at the sharp iron spikes of the high, rusty gate.

"I don't like the idea of climbing over that gate. There must be an easier way to get in," Nancy said, her gaze roving along the crumbling, ivy-covered wall.

"I'll not attempt to climb over any part of it," announced Bess with finality. "I have on a good dress."

"Then you'll be left behind," George told her cousin tersely.

She and Nancy examined the stone wall. Some distance along, it was a bit lower than the gate and offered good toe holds. It was not difficult for the girls to grasp the vines and pull themselves to the top. Bess finally decided to follow. Leaping down lightly from the wall, the three friends started through the dense growth of trees and shrubs.

As they progressed, Bess felt rather uneasy. Beneath the canopy of leaves it was damp and cool, but there were many strange noises to unnerve her.

"Listen!" she commanded tensely. "What's that?"

Nancy and George could hear the sound plainly, but

for a moment they could not identify it. Then Nancy smiled.

"The cooing of a pigeon!" she explained. "Come along, or we'll all have the jitters."

Before long, Bess had a bad case of jitters, bordering on real fear. She walked directly into a spider web and as she was exclaiming "Ugh!" and brushing it from her mouth, something furry shot in front of her. She gave a little scream.

"What's the matter?" cried Nancy, turning back.

Her eyes opened wide as she caught sight of an enormous rat scurrying through the underbrush.

"They—they bite," said Bess. "I don't like this place. Let's turn back."

"Not I," replied Nancy, stalking on. "This place is intriguing. And if it's going to solve a mystery——"

"It won't solve any," argued Bess. "But it could make them, all right!"

"Watch where you're walking and you'll be safe," advised George, somewhat annoyed.

Just ahead stretched a long avenue of oak trees which gave prospect of leading to the castle. Tramping through waist-high grass, the girls came first to a vine-tangled, fern-matted bower. Two handsome stone vases lay on their sides, cracked from having filled with water which had frozen during the winter.

"What a shame this place is being neglected," Nancy commented, pausing a moment. "Mr. Keep ought to take care of it. If Florianna should come back, she would hardly recognize it, I'm sure."

At the end of the oak-lined avenue the girls came to a weather-stained loggia of stone. Its four handsomely carved pillars rose to support a balcony over which vines trailed. Steps led to the upper part.

Mounting to the balcony, Nancy and her friends obtained a fine view of the near-by gardens. They had been laid out in formal sections, each one bounded by a stone wall or a hedge. Here and there were small circular pools, now heavy with lichens and moss, and fountains with leaf-filled basins.

"We still haven't located the castle," Nancy remarked, starting on again. "Let's cross that bridge over there and try that trail."

She pointed to a rustic bridge which spanned a stream so clogged with water lilies that there scarcely was any space between them.

"This old bridge is pretty rickety," George complained as they started across it. "Think it will hold our weight?"

"I'll go ahead and try it," Nancy offered.

The bridge swayed and groaned as she cautiously crossed to the opposite side. It held her, however, so George and Bess followed in single file.

"I wonder where this leads?" Nancy said, staring at a slippery, moss-grown stone walk.

On a rotted post near by was a rustic sign with carved letters. The Drew girl stepped closer to look at the words.

"'The Haunted Walk,'" she read aloud.

"Let's try another trail," Bess said with a shiver. "This garden is spooky enough without deliberately inviting a meeting with ghosts!"

"Oh, come along," Nancy laughed, taking her friend firmly by the arm. "It's only a name. Besides, the walk may lead to something interesting."

"That's just what I'm afraid of," Bess retorted, but she allowed herself to be persuaded.

Spreading lilac bushes canopied the trail. Their branches caught at Nancy's hair and clutched at her clothing. Impatiently, she thrust them back, or held the shrubs for her friends to pass beneath.

"I wish we'd gone the other way," Bess complained. "This is no fun."

"I think it is," Nancy replied. "It's so mysterious here! It's so——"

Her voice trailed away. At the sudden pause, George and Bess glanced at her quickly. Nancy was staring directly toward a giant evergreen.

"What is it?" Bess demanded fearfully. "What do you see?"

"Why, nothing."

"You didn't act as if it were nothing," George commented.

"I thought I saw something, but I must have been mistaken."

Despite their coaxing, Nancy would not reveal what had startled her. In truth, she was not certain just what she had seen. For an instant a pair of penetrating, human eyes had seemed to stare at her from behind the evergreen. Then the eyes had blinked shut and vanished.

"It must have been my imagination," Nancy told herself. "Or possibly I saw an animal."

She walked on hurriedly. Sensing her thoughts, Bess and George drew closer to her.

Nancy rounded the evergreen and saw that it hid a fallen-down, decayed summerhouse. She stopped short, struck by the realization that someone had been lurking there only a moment before. Those burning eyes had *not* been a figment of her imagination.

"Now what do you see?" George asked in a low tone.

Nancy decided to keep her secret no longer. In a whisper she confided that she believed someone had been hiding in the summerhouse, perhaps watching their movements.

"I knew we shouldn't have chosen this walk," Bess muttered. "It *is* haunted."

"Haunted by a human being," Nancy said grimly. "I wish I knew who it was that was spying on us."

There was no sign of anyone in or near the summerhouse now. And the girls heard neither the rustle of leaves nor the pad of retreating footsteps.

"Let's go back to the car," Bess proposed suddenly. "We've seen enough of this place."

"I haven't," corrected Nancy. "I'm getting more curious every minute."

Not far from the summerhouse was a stone wall. It occurred to Nancy that the person who had observed them might have scrambled over it to avoid detection. She announced her intention of climbing up to make sure.

"Don't do it!" Bess pleaded nervously. "After all, we've no right to be on this property. Let's go."

Nancy was not to be deterred. While Bess and George watched uneasily, she scrambled up the vine-covered wall. Weathered stone crumbled beneath her fingers. Before she gained a hold on the ledge, she slipped and nearly fell.

"Do be careful, Nancy," Bess warned her. "There are sharp rocks just beneath you, and goodness only knows what's on top of that wall."

Indeed, Nancy was in danger. Agile though she was, she did not have the strength to swing herself atop the wall. Her arms were tiring, and she could feel the soft rock loosening under the pressure of her fingers.

"Can't make it," she gasped.

George started to reply, but the words froze on her lips. Bess, too, was struck speechless with terror.

On the ledge overhead was a huge, venomous snake, its head raised. It was about to bury its fangs in Nancy's up-stretched hand!

Chapter V

BEYOND THE WALL

NANCY could not see the snake. Bess was so horrified she could not speak. It was George who found her voice, crying out sharply:

"Let go, Nancy! Quick!"

Startled, the Drew girl released her hold on the crumbling wall and dropped to the ground. Picking herself up, she gazed questioningly at the girls.

"Just s-see what was making for you!" Bess quavered, still shaken from the close call her friend had had.

Dramatically she pointed to the huge snake. At sight of it, Nancy shuddered involuntarily. Though a bite from the copperhead would not have been fatal to one in such good health as herself, it would have been painful and required medical attention.

"Oh, George, you saved me!" she thanked her friend appreciatively. "I should have been more careful. Guess I'd better not climb the wall."

"Those are the most sensible words I've heard you say today!" Bess declared with feeling. "Let's get away from the Haunted Walk before we find ourselves in real trouble."

"Yes, let's go back to the car," George added. "I have an appointment in town, and anyway, it may rain."

Nancy was reluctant to leave the estate without seeing Heath Castle, but she noticed that clouds were darkening the sky.

"All right," she agreed. "But let's come back soon."

They retraced their way across the creaking bridge. Try as they would, they could not find the right direction to the main road.

"We're probably a long way from the car," George said finally. "I'll climb a tree and see if I can spot it."

"Keep an eye out for snakes," Bess advised as she gave her cousin a boost up the trunk of a giant sugar maple.

George was as nimble as a monkey. Climbing high among the branches, she shouted that the river was close by, the road far away.

"We've wandered a long distance from the car," the girl reported discouragingly.

George slid down the tree, pointing out the route they must take to reach the parked automobile.

"We'll cut straight through that woods ahead," she announced.

"Are you sure we won't get lost?" Bess asked doubtfully.

"Just follow little George."

Nancy and Bess were quite willing to have her lead the way. She pushed confidently ahead, tramping down the high grass and thrusting aside thorny bushes. But as the going became more difficult, her pace slackened.

B

"I hope you know where you're leading us," Nancy said at last. "It seems to me we're moving in a wide circle."

George paused to catch her breath. Her gloomy silence confirmed Nancy's suspicion.

"George, are we lost?" she asked.

"I don't know about you," the girl answered ruefully. "Myself—yes."

"It's going to rain any minute, too," Bess said, sinking down on a mossy log. "Oh, why did we come to this horrible, gloomy place? Imagine anyone building a home here."

"If the roads were opened and some shrubs cut down, the estate would be very lovely," Nancy pointed out. "I'd like to live here myself."

After resting a few minutes, the girls took a vote on what to do, and decided to continue on through the woods. Nancy was chosen leader, and proved a better pathfinder than George. Before long she came to some trampled grass.

"Now I know where we are!" she cried jubilantly. "We're near the estate boundary."

A few hundred feet farther on they saw the wall itself and scrambled over it, reaching the shelter of the car just as the first raindrops splashed against the windshield. Fortunately, Nancy was able to get to the paved highway before the side road became a mire of mud.

"Let's wear old clothes next time we go to Heath Castle," she said to Bess and George, as the girls parted company in River Heights.

"And take along snake serum, axes, and lunch," advised George pointedly.

Alone, Nancy suddenly recalled that she had invited Lieutenant Masters to dinner at the Drew home that evening. At seven o'clock the attractive officer arrived, not wearing a uniform, but looking very feminine and pretty in a blue lace dress.

As dinner progressed, Nancy knew from her father's chuckles and the quick repartee that he was enjoying their guest immensely. After a time the talk became more serious as mention was made of several famous court cases. Nancy brought up the problem of the Fenimores and the mystery of Florianna and Heath Castle.

"I thought that mysterious place would interest you," young Lieutenant Masters said, smiling. "By this time I suppose you've been to the courthouse, too, and read the Heath will."

"Why, no," Nancy confessed. "So far I've confined my investigations to the estate. Have you read the will?"

"No, I've never had time to examine it."

"Why not do it together?" Nancy proposed eagerly.

To this the policewoman promptly agreed, saying that ten o'clock the next morning would be a convenient time for her to meet the girl at the courthouse.

Since Nancy was familiar with legal terms, having read many of her father's papers, the Walter Heath document was easy for her to decipher. Hector Keep was named as sole executor.

A quick reading confirmed the story that the entire Heath estate had been bequeathed to Florianna, also known as Flossie Johnson. In the event the estate was not claimed by her within five years of Walter Heath's death, the property was to go to the county for a park.

One clause in the will held Nancy's attention. It read:

"It is my belief and hope that Florianna still lives and will claim the property within the allotted time. She will be able to identify herself in a special way, thus insuring that no impostor can receive my estate."

"I wonder what that means?" Nancy mused, pointing it out to Lieutenant Masters, who was equally puzzled.

"I haven't the least idea," said the officer.

They went over the document again, but it gave no clue to the special means by which Florianna might establish her identity. Thinking that the dancer's sister, Mrs. Fenimore, might know the answer, they drove to her cottage.

The invalid, her face pale, was sitting on the shabby front porch. She was trying without much success to patch a sunsuit of Joan's.

"Good morning," Mrs. Fenimore greeted the visitors

wanly. She stared anxiously at the policewoman. "It's—it's not Joan again?"

"No, it isn't. I'm happy to report that your little girl is behaving very well. We came to ask you a few questions about your sister Florianna."

The invalid relaxed but spoke wearily. "I'll tell you everything I can. Long ago I gave up hope that she ever will be found."

"Then you believe that your sister may not be living?" Nancy interposed soberly.

"No, Flossie must be alive," Mrs. Fenimore replied with quiet conviction. "Otherwise, in all these years I would have had some word of her death."

"Tell us about your sister," urged Lieutenant Masters kindly. "She was younger than you?"

"No, Flossie was seven years older. Our parents died when we were very young, and we lived with an aunt who was pretty strict. I never minded Aunt Matilda's scoldings, but Flossie was high-strung. She took dancing lessons secretly, and when Aunt Matilda punished her for it, she ran away.

"For several years Flossie danced wherever she could get an engagement and studied during her spare moments. She changed her name to Florianna. Oh, she worked hard! I never saw anyone more determined to get on in the world."

"You saw Florianna often after she became famous?" inquired Lieutenant Masters.

"Only now and then. But she wrote to me every week without fail. I was so excited when she became engaged to Walter Heath. It was a secret, so of course I told no one."

"You have no idea why your sister went away?" asked Nancy.

"She needed a rest. That's all I know. Flossie didn't tell anyone her plans." The speaker's voice had become soft and dreamy.

"Could anything have happened between Florianna and Walter Heath to make her unhappy enough to disappear?" speculated Nancy.

Mrs. Fenimore shook her head. "Florianna never hinted

of such a thing. She was beautiful and talented. He was handsome, wealthy, and very kind. They adored each other. No, I am sure he had nothing to do with her disappearance."

Mention of the deceased estate owner reminded Nancy of the real purpose of her call. Accordingly, she asked Mrs. Fenimore about the strange identification clause in the Heath will.

"I wondered myself what that meant when I read it," the invalid replied. "The only thing I could figure out was that Walt and Florianna must have shared a secret."

"Do you think Hector Keep might know what it was?" Nancy asked.

Mrs. Fenimore's face darkened. "Please don't mention that man's name!" she requested sharply.

"Don't you like him?"

"I detest him. All these years he's pretended to search for Florianna."

"Pretended?"

"Well, I can't prove it, but I'm sure he's not honest. From the beginning he assumed that Florianna was dead. He made only half-hearted attempts to find her. Now he doesn't even try, and——"

Mrs. Fenimore suddenly slumped in her chair. Both Nancy and the policewoman jumped forward to catch her as she fainted.

"Water!" said the lieutenant tersely. "This has been too much for her!"

Nancy flew to the kitchen of the little house, returning a moment later with a glass of water. The policewoman had laid the inert victim on the floor of the porch, and was taking her pulse. Now she whisked a tiny first-aid kit from her pocket, crushed a tablet from it in the palm of her hand, and held it to Mrs. Fenimore's nostrils. In a moment the invalid revived and was given the water to drink.

"It was foolish of me to faint," she said as they assisted her to the couch in the living room.

"Perhaps we'd better not talk any more today," suggested Nancy.

"I'm all right now," Mrs. Fenimore insisted. "I'd like to talk. Isn't there something we can do to find my sister?" she asked pitifully. "The time's getting so short. In less than three weeks the estate will go to the county. I don't care about myself, but Joan needs so many things that Florianna could give her."

"Surely there must be some clue to her whereabouts," Nancy said thoughtfully. "A clever person should be able to find your sister."

"If only someone would make an honest effort!" Mrs. Fenimore's voice became pleading. "Won't you help me, Miss Drew?"

"I'm afraid it's too big a job for me."

"Oh, no it isn't!" Mrs. Fenimore insisted. "I've read about your work. You're the very one to find my sister."

"I hardly know what to say," Nancy demurred, glancing toward the policewoman.

Lieutenant Masters gazed at the girl with a challenging smile.

"Why not say yes?" she asked softly. "From the first I've known that this was a case for you. If you work fast, you may find Florianna in time to save Heath Castle."

Chapter VI

EXPLORING THE INLET

NANCY promised Mrs. Fenimore that she would do everything she could to trace her missing sister. Secretly, she wondered whether she would be able to find the dancer in time to save Heath Castle for her.

"May I see a photograph of your sister?" she requested.

"I have a number of excellent ones," Mrs. Fenimore replied eagerly. "They're in the drawer of that table."

At her direction Nancy got them. There were six, taken

years before when the dancer was at the height of her career. Several were inscribed with her name and a greeting. The face was a distinctive one. Carefully Nancy noted the perfect features, the beautiful dark eyes, the straight nose and firm chin.

"Florianna doubtless has changed a great deal since last I saw her," Mrs. Fenimore remarked. "I can't seem to realize that ten years have slipped by."

"Your sister is lovely," Nancy commented. "Joan looks a little like her."

"Yes, she does. And certainly my daughter has Flossie's vivacious ways," the woman replied. "She's quite a little actress. Maybe some day——"

As the invalid looked dreamily into space, Nancy was afraid she might faint again. Fortunately, Mrs. Fenimore regained control of herself. Lieutenant Masters, fearing the conversation had upset the woman, said they must leave.

"Please try not to worry," the Drew girl urged Mrs. Fenimore. "I'll start working at once on the mystery."

When she and the woman police officer reached the automobile, Nancy declined a ride, saying she would like to walk and think about how she would start solving the strange case. The lieutenant wished her luck.

"Call on me any time I can help you," the young woman urged as she drove off.

Nancy wandered up the street. Children were coming home from school to luncheon. Some of them smiled in a friendly way at the girl, but many of them were rude.

"It's too bad Joan has to live in this neighbourhood," Nancy thought. "I wonder——"

At this moment she spied the child playing with an older boy in a vacant lot. They were tossing a ball for a stray dog to retrieve.

"That boy looks familiar," Nancy thought. "Where have I seen him before?"

Suddenly the boy in a fit of temper hit the dog with a stick. Joan screamed.

"You ugly mean brute!" he shouted. "You're chewing my ball to pieces!"

Nancy paused. "Stop that!" she ordered. "Is that a nice way to treat a dog? He hasn't hurt your ball. He was only playing."

The boy, who was ragged and dirty, gazed at her with hard, unfriendly eyes.

"Is he your dog?" he asked impudently.

"Why, no."

"Then it's none of your business if I hit him! I'll do it as often as I please! So!"

Nancy started to reply, but it was not necessary. The dog dropped the ball and slunk off. The boy picked it up. Giving the girl a baleful look, he too went on his way.

Nancy, taking Joan by the hand, led her off. As tactfully as possible, she suggested that the child ought to find a girl playmate in the neighbourhood.

"Jeddy Hooker's the only one that lives close to me," Joan replied, skipping happily along beside her companion. "I don't like him when he's cruel like today, but most of the time he's lots of fun. He always thinks up things to do."

"Why didn't you go right home to lunch?" Nancy asked. "Your mother is waiting for you."

Joan hung her head. "There's nothing good in the house to eat."

Nancy turned into a store, bought some sandwiches and milk and told the child to take them home at once for her mother and herself.

"Oh, thank you, Nancy Drew," Joan beamed. "And—and I won't play with Jeddy any more if you don't want me to."

"That's a good girl."

"And please try to find my aunt for me."

"I will," promised Nancy, starting in the other direction. Until they were out of sight of each other, Nancy and Joan continued to turn around and wave. Nancy was sure she had made a firm friend of the little girl.

"I'm not very far from Mehearty's," the young detective thought presently. "I believe I'll go there and find out if he's seen that man who crashed into my boat."

She turned down a side street and in a little while came to the clam digger's home. The old sailor was on the shore repairing his rowboat.

"Well now, me lass, I'm glad to see ye," the old sailor said. "But I'm afeered I haven't got good news for ye."

"You mean about the boat?"

"I've looked high and low for that damaged boat," the old man told the girl regretfully. "It's not tied up anywhere along here."

"How about the inlet?" asked Nancy.

Mehearty admitted that he had not been there. "Too busy," he explained. "Maybe I'll go this very afternoon. I need a mess o' clams and there might be some up the inlet. Ye want to come along? I'll show ye the Heath factory if ye want to see it."

For Nancy the opportunity was one not to be overlooked. Despite her misadventure of a few days before, she was eager to visit the spot.

"Just tell me when to be here," she accepted eagerly. To his reply of three o'clock, she added, "I'll bring along one of my friends."

Nancy hurried home, ate some lunch, and telephoned to George. Promptly at three o'clock the two girls met Mehearty at the waterfront.

"I'll put ye to work," he chuckled, as he gathered together his fishing and clamming equipment, and asked them to help him load it into his rowboat.

Presently they were swimming along the tranquil waters of the Muskoka River at a rapid rate, for the old man had muscles of iron. Behind the craft there trailed a long copper wire which gleamed in the sunlight.

"I'm trollin' for my dinner tonight," Mehearty explained. "There's somethin' yankin' on 'er now, I do believe!"

Resting the oars, the old man pulled steadily on the line. A four-pound bass flopped into the boat, wriggled from his grasp, and landed in George's lap.

"Oh!" she exclaimed, jumping up and brushing water from her dress as Mehearty apologetically took the fish.

While the girls kept the boat from drifting downstream, the man removed the fish from the hook and dropped it into his basket. Then he wound up the copper troll line and put it away.

"Fishin's not much good in the inlet," he remarked. "But we'll find clams there."

The upper river was very still. As the little boat slipped into the inlet sometime later, there was no sound save the occasional chirping of a bird. Hunching low now and then to avoid the overhanging bushes, Nancy watched the coves for hidden boats. There were none and there was nothing to indicate that anyone had been near the inlet for weeks.

"It don't look as if we're goin' to find your friend," Mehearty remarked after he had rowed a quarter of a mile up the stream. "We're nearly to Heath's button factory now. I'll anchor here."

The old man had located a bed of clams in the shallow water. Asking the girls to balance his woven basket on the gunwale, he waded in to dig the clams out of the mud and sand. As he tossed them, some landed in the basket, others the girls caught and threw in. All the time Mehearty kept singing snatches of familiar sea songs, but each one ended with:

> "Clams by the bushel,
> Clams by the lot,
> Clams for the kettle,
> Clams for the pot."

"Basket's full," Nancy called in a few minutes.

As George caught the last one, she held it in her hand to examine it. The clam looked different from the others. The next instant she stared in astonishment at an ugly purple stain on her fingers. Her dress looked as if it had been splattered with dye.

"Goodness!" she exclaimed in dismay. "Where did that come from?"

Mehearty splashed over to the boat. He looked surprised when he saw George's stained hands.

"That purple colour is a dye," he explained. "It came from this here whelk."

"So this kind of mollusk is called a whelk?" Nancy asked.

"That's right," Mehearty replied.

It was not the shell, he told the girls, but the body of the animal inside that produced the dye.

"Real dye?" Nancy inquired, deeply impressed.

"The very best to be had. Whelks have been used for dye makin' ever since ancient times. Used with purpuras or dog whelks, they make the finest dye ever. This here whelk is the kind ye can eat, too."

"I'll not try eating any," said George with a grimace. She attempted without success to wash the stain from her fingers. "Is it difficult to make the dye?"

"Anyone can do it. Ye break open the shells and remove the little animals. Soak 'em in salt water for a few days, then boil 'em in a lead kettle until ye have a pale green liquid."

"Green?" Nancy asked in surprise.

"Yes'm, the liquid is green, but when ye dip wool into it, it comes out purple."

"I'll buy my clothes already dyed," George said, grinning ruefully. "Whelks aren't used commercially here at River Heights, are they?"

"Never heard of anyone goin' into the business. Whelks ain't plentiful enough around here."

Mehearty got into the boat and started off again. As they rounded a bend, the girls saw a large, square building set some distance back from shore. The banks near by were littered with discarded bits of clam shells.

"That's the Heath button factory," Mehearty identified the place. "She's sure gone to pieces since I was here last."

Nancy gazed curiously at the neglected, brick structure. Vines lay thick on the shingle roof and all the windows were broken.

Not expecting to find anyone around, she was surprised to see figures close to the factory entrance. Two men were visible for an instant. Then they vanished, and Nancy was certain they had gone into the building. Before she could mention what she had seen, Mehearty pointed to something hidden near some bushes.

"A boat!" he exclaimed. "And her prow's smashed, too!"

The bow of the boat had been drawn up on the sand. At a glance George and Nancy identified it as the blue and white painted craft that had struck them.

"Oh, Mehearty, please pull in here," Nancy requested excitedly.

"Is that the boat ye're lookin' for?" the old sailor asked, resting his oars.

Without replying, Nancy leaped out, splashing through knee-deep water to shore. Not to be left behind, George followed close at her heels.

"Hey, where ye gals goin' in such a rush?" Mehearty called after them.

Nancy paused, suddenly realizing that it might be wise to proceed with caution. Tersely she explained to the old clam digger that she had just seen two men disappear into the button factory. Maybe they owned the boat!

"Hmph!" Mehearty grunted. "Well, I'll bet ye a mess o'clams they ain't got no right in there!"

"I want to talk to them," Nancy called. "Mehearty, will you stay here near the damaged boat? If the men come, try to hold them until we get back."

The sailor did not like the inactive role assigned to him, but before he could protest, the girls had gone.

Chapter VII

A MYSTERIOUS EXPLOSION

NANCY and George had to cross a stretch of low, marshy land in order to reach the old button factory. Their shoes, already water-soaked, became caked with mud. But the girls were deeply grateful for the high, wild grass that screened their approach from anyone who might look in their direction.

"I'm sure those two men went into the building," Nancy stated as they moved closer. "One of them wore a cap like the fellow who crashed into our motorboat."

"And the other?" George inquired. "Do you know him?"

"I caught only a fleeting glimpse of him," Nancy replied vaguely.

Actually she thought that he resembled the lawyer, Hector Keep. Not being certain, she was reluctant to give a definite answer.

While still twenty yards from the factory, the girls were startled to hear the sound of hammering. The pounding noise came from inside the building.

"Those men are in there, just as I thought," Nancy said, cautiously pulling aside the tall grass to obtain a clear view of the building. "What are they doing, I wonder?"

"Workmen sent to repair the place, perhaps," was George's reply.

Nancy offered no comment. It was entirely possible that Hector Keep had brought another man to the property either to inspect it, or to do some work, though she seriously doubted this.

As the girls moved closer, the hammering ceased. Though they waited several minutes, it was not resumed.

"We may have been seen," Nancy said uncertainly. "I hope the men haven't left."

Pushing through to the end of the marsh, the girls saw that the front door to the factory stood open. Nancy peered inside. A long corridor opened into several offices and led to a large work room at the back. No one was in sight.

As the girls started along the hallway, they heard retreating footsteps. Glancing out of one of the dirt-smudged windows, they saw two men running in the direction of the river.

"Oh, Nancy!" George cried. "They must have heard us!"

"They're going toward the boat!" added Nancy excitedly. Already the men were well hidden by the high marsh grass. The girls ran quickly toward a rear door. As they neared it, deafening sounds of an explosion filled the air. The walls of the factory rocked and plaster tumbled down.

"Nancy!" George cried frantically.

She lurched backward just in time to avoid being crushed by a heavy falling beam. A board struck her on the forehead, slightly dazing her.

"Nancy!" she called weakly. "Nancy!"

There was no answering cry. To George's horror she saw that a huge pile of debris had separated her from her chum. One whole corridor wall had caved in.

Nancy must be buried beneath it!

"Nancy! Nancy!" George shouted again, struggling to her feet.

The air was thick with plaster dust, but she paid no heed. Coughing and choking, she frantically began pulling away boards and chunks of plaster.

In the meantime the two strangers, who had paused in the tall grass, were just about to go back to the factory when they heard running footsteps. Mehearty, fearful upon hearing the explosion, was racing toward the factory, clam rake over his shoulder. He passed within a few feet of the men.

"Oh dear, oh dear," he kept mumbling, "I hope nothin's happened to the lassies!"

He found George still working feverishly at the pile of debris.

"Mehearty!" the girl cried. "I can't find Nancy! She must be buried under the wreckage!"

The old man's worst fears were confirmed! He said nothing, but began raking furiously at the pile of plaster that blocked the corridor.

At this very moment Nancy was lying stunned on the floor of a little room some distance from where the others were working. The force of the explosion had lifted the girl off her feet and hurled her into a storage closet. Then the door had slammed shut and the ceiling above it, in falling, had sealed the entrance.

As she regained consciousness, Nancy found herself in

total darkness and wondered where she was. Slowly the confused girl got to her feet and felt around her prison. At last she found a door and tried it. It would not budge, and there was no other exit.

"What'll I do?" she thought, still a bit dazed by the blast.

In a few minutes Nancy's mind cleared. She knew she was bruised and that there was a mean scratch on her arm. But she paid no attention to these. She must get out!

And where was George, the distracted girl worried. Then suddenly Nancy thought she heard her name called. The sound was far, far away.

Was it George's voice?

With all her strength Nancy pounded on the door and pushed her body against it. At last it yielded ever so slightly. Through the crack she shouted:

"George!"

"Nancy! Where are you?" came a muffled reply.

George was safe! This knowledge renewed Nancy's strength. She gave the door a mighty heave and it yielded about two inches. She called out:

"Here I am! In the closet!"

Mehearty and George leaped across the rubble. With the rake, and their hands and feet, they cleared away enough of the debris to free Nancy. As she squeezed herself from her prison, Mehearty mumbled:

"Thank goodness, ye're alive!"

George embraced her friend in excited relief. "Oh, I was so scared," she said. Then soberly she added, "Why didn't you answer when I called you twenty minutes ago?"

"I didn't hear you," the Drew girl replied ruefully.

"Knocked out?" asked Mehearty, gazing intently at Nancy to be sure she was all right.

"I'm afraid I was. But I'm none the worse for it. What caused the explosion?" Suddenly she recalled the two strangers who had run from the building. "What became of those two men?"

George had forgotten about them during the excitement.

Recalling that she last had seen the pair hastening toward the river, she asked Mehearty if he had observed anyone.

"Nary a soul," he responded.

Nancy, George, and the old clam digger plunged through the marsh grass toward the river bank. The damaged motorboat no longer was there.

"Those rascals sneaked away, drat 'em," Mehearty muttered in disgust. "Do ye think that makes 'em guilty, Miss Nancy?"

"Guilty on two counts," the girl replied. "Guilty of damaging the boat I rented, and guilty of causing the explosion."

"But why cause an explosion?" asked George.

Nancy shrugged. She did not want to mention any of her theories just yet, but an idea had come to her. One of the men had resembled Hector Keep. The lawyer's actions were becoming very suspicious. He actually had been accused by Mrs. Fenimore of not being honest. The man certainly had neglected to take care of the Heath gardens and the factory. The whole thing looked bad for him.

"But what could be his reason for wanting to destroy the factory?" Nancy mused.

She was brought out of her reverie by George, who suggested that they go home.

"The fellow with the damaged boat is gone," she reminded her friend. "Since we came here to find him, we may as well leave."

During the trip back to Mehearty's, the clam digger and the girls kept their eyes open for the blue and white motorboat. But they saw no sign of it.

"I'll be glad to take ye on a trip again," the old sailor offered when they reached the dock at River Heights.

Nancy thanked the man. On the way home she was very thoughtful, and could hardly wait for the moment when she could talk to her father in the library after dinner. For half an hour she expounded her theories regarding the mystery of the Heath estate.

"But why would Keep want to damage property he's paid

to look after?" asked Mr. Drew, when he had heard the story. "It doesn't make sense to me."

"I'm sure there's a great deal more to the Heath case than Florianna's disappearance," Nancy declared. "Take the explosion today, for example. It wasn't just an accident. There may be something pretty sinister back of it all."

"I'll agree with you on that point," Mr. Drew said soberly. "Nancy, I know it's useless to ask you to give up trying to solve a mystery——"

"Oh, it is, Dad!"

"At least I can ask you to be careful. Remember, you're my one and only daughter."

"I'll keep it in mind," she said, hugging him affectionately. "Now, about the Heath affair. Isn't it possible that someone is prowling around the property in the hope of discovering the clue Walter Heath mentioned in his will?"

"You mean the one by which Florianna can identify herself beyond all doubt?"

"Yes, Dad. If an impostor should stumble upon that clue, it would be an easy matter for him to have some woman claim the fortune."

"Not so easy as you may think, Nancy. A number of persons knew Florianna."

"But in all these years she could have changed so much that no one would recognize her."

"True. I follow your reasoning. Nevertheless, any person who put in a claim would have to satisfy Hector Keep and the court that it was a just one."

Nancy gazed steadily at her father. "Do you think Hector Keep would be difficult to satisfy? If he isn't honest——"

Mr. Drew squirmed in his chair.

"Nancy, I don't like to think the man would take a bribe, if that's what you're hinting," he said. "You know my opinion of Keep. I don't like his methods in handling law cases, but I can't prove he's actually done anything dishonest."

"You admit that the Heath case looks suspicious?" the girl pressed him.

"Yes, I do, Nancy. And you have my full approval to work on it; that is, to try to find Florianna. The rest of it you'd better leave alone."

"I've mulled over it a lot," the girl went on, "I've even thought that maybe Florianna is being held a prisoner somewhere."

Mr. Drew looked surprised. "In the castle?" he asked.

"Who knows?" his daughter bantered. "But seriously, I hardly know where to begin my investigation. The explosion today kind of changed my plans."

"How do you mean?"

"I heard that Walter Heath made scientific experiments at the castle. If Hector Keep suspects there's a secret somewhere within those crumbling walls——"

Mr. Drew gazed at his daughter with sudden suspicion. "Young lady, you're leading up to something!" he accused her with a twinkle in his eye. "Out with it!"

"I'm only trying to arouse your interest, Dad," confessed Nancy with a gay laugh. "Why not go to the factory with me? You may find a clue I've overlooked."

"And be blown to bits?" asked Mr. Drew. "No, thank you."

"I need your help, Dad," Nancy coaxed.

"Well, if you put it that way," said her father, weakening. "Actually, I haven't the time to spare, but I will go to please you."

"Tomorrow morning then."

"So soon?"

"Time is short, and I must solve the mystery within three weeks."

Chapter VIII

NO TRESPASSERS ALLOWED

NANCY and her father were up early the next morning. Without troubling Mrs. Gruen, they hastily made breakfast and drove to the damaged button factory. The last half mile was not easy riding, for the road, like everything else on the Heath property, was in bad condition.

"I see why those men came by boat," said Mr. Drew, finally stopping the car some distance from the building. "This road is pretty hard on tyres. We'll walk from here."

Nancy led the way through the dew-laden grass to the scene of the explosion. There was no sign of anyone near the factory. The only sound to be heard was the wild cry of a huge water fowl which rose from the marsh.

"Those two fellows did a good job of destruction," commented the lawyer as the Drews cautiously entered the building.

"Here's where the wall caved in near George and me," Nancy explained, kicking at the debris with her foot.

"Looks as if it might have been dynamited," her father remarked after gazing about carefully. "Let's see if we can find any telltale evidence."

For the next half-hour father and daughter scrambled in and out of the rubble. Discovering nothing of importance in the corridor, they decided to investigate the large workroom at the back. It was necessary for them to go outside and climb in through a window to reach the room, because the inside doorway to it was blocked.

"Oh, it's like a ghost town," said Nancy, as she surveyed the rusted machinery and layers of dust. "To think that this once was a prosperous factory!"

"It isn't much of a tribute to the Heaths, I'll admit," commented Mr. Drew.

"What was this machine used for?" Nancy asked, interested in a steel saw attached to it.

"This is for cutting," her father explained, pausing beside it. "The clam shell is placed in the machine. An operator moves a lever and down comes the circular steel saw. Presto! A little shell disk drops into the hopper. Another machine slices the disc into pieces of uniform thickness, and there you have some buttons!"

"How clever!" said Nancy.

"The buttons pass through still another machine which polishes them," Mr. Drew went on. "In the last operation thread-holes are drilled through them."

"To think all this was done right here in River Heights and I never knew anything about it," Nancy said in wonder.

Mr. Drew turned away. "I guess there's nothing more to learn, Nancy, either about the buttons or the mystery of the factory. If those men deliberately caused the explosion, they skilfully covered their work. We may as well leave before we're accused of trespassing."

Bitterly disappointed, Nancy was just about to let her father help her through the window, when her sharp eyes caught sight of something.

"Dad! Look!" she cried.

Sticking out from a corner of the rubble in the doorway lay a scrap of paper, and near it were several freshly made footprints. Nancy darted toward them, and picked up the paper.

A glance sufficed to show her that the words on it might have value. The sheet had been torn in such a way that only part of the message was there. It was written in a man's hand and read:

> Dear C,
>   Some
> cret which I
> in a wall
> famous
> worthy

Nancy showed her father what she had found.

"Interesting," he commented, scanning the torn paper. "But I can't say that it makes much sense. The footprints might be a better clue."

He stooped to examine them. "Freshly made without a doubt," he said. "Evidently your two strangers have visited here since the explosion!"

"Then that practically proves they're searching for something," Nancy concluded. "Something they think was hidden and could be found only by blasting it out."

"If that's true, I'm sure it has nothing to do with Florianna," said Mr. Drew.

"Maybe not," Nancy sighed. She was staring at the torn note. "I believe I've stumbled on a worth-while clue just the same," she said slowly. "I can guess now that one of these words is 'secret.'"

She pocketed the message and reluctantly left the factory with her father, who had an appointment at his office and already was late. At home again, she spent more than an hour trying to piece together the missing words of the note. Who had written them? The paper appeared old, the ink slightly faded.

"It wouldn't surprise me if Walter Heath wrote the message," she said to Hannah Gruen. "No way to prove it, though."

"I know how you might find out," was the housekeeper's surprising answer.

"How?"

"Walter Heath was a member of the River Heights Historical Society before his death. Isn't it likely the society would have specimens of his handwriting?"

"Hannah Gruen, you're a genius!" Nancy cried, giving the woman a hug. "I'm off to the Historical Society building this very minute!"

Luck was with her. On many of the books and pieces of furniture which Walter Heath had given to the museum she found not one, but several samples of the deceased estate owner's handwriting.

"It's the same as that in the note!" Nancy decided excitedly, comparing the script. "Now, if only I can find the missing half of the note!"

Many questions plagued the girl. Had the torn sheet fallen from some niche in the wall at the time of the explosion? Or had one of the strangers dropped it when leaving the ruins?

"Hector Keep may have the other part," Nancy speculated. "If so, I'm afraid I'll never see it."

Seeking her father's aid once more, Nancy asked him to talk to the lawyer and try to get what information he could from him about the Heath case. Again she was to be disappointed.

"Mr. Keep came honestly by his name," Carson Drew reported somewhat later to his daughter. "He certainly kept his secrets from me!"

"Didn't he tell you anything?" Nancy asked.

"Nothing worth mentioning. As soon as I spoke of Heath Castle and the button factory, he closed up as tight as one of Mehearty's clams!"

"Did you mention Florianna's name?"

"Yes. Hector Keep stressed that he was still searching diligently for her."

"I wonder," said Nancy softly.

The Heath Castle mystery was no nearer a solution than before. Eager as the girl was to revisit the estate, she found it impossible, because her father had made her promise not to go there alone; and none of her friends would be free to accompany her until the next day.

"I know what I'll do," she thought enthusiastically. "Go over the whole Heath property by plane."

For some time Nancy had been taking flying lessons whenever it was possible. She had not soloed yet, but hoped to do so very soon. Telephoning to her instructor, she made an appointment.

"I wondered when I was going to hear from you again," the young man said, as the two climbed into his plane. "Have you been busy solving a new mystery?"

"There's a new mystery bothering me right now," laughed Nancy. "How to work all these gadgets."

Despite her words, she started the motor and headed the plane into the wind as if she were a seasoned pilot. Reaching sufficient altitude, she banked and headed in the direction of Heath Castle.

"When I get home I'll map the area," she thought, making careful mental notes as she flew over the estate. "At least I have a good idea now where the castle is situated."

Nancy circled the area several times. Satisfied that she could jot down a general plan of the place, she started to leave. Suddenly the girl noticed a cloud of smoke in the vicinity of the castle. Curious, she banked the plane and flew back over the estate. The smoke was rising in a mass, but Nancy could not make out its exact origin, because the foliage was so dense.

"Someone is on the estate, anyway," she mused. "Oh, dear, I hope the fire won't do any damage."

The plane nosed downward, reminding the girl that she must pay close attention to her piloting. For the first time her instructor spoke to her. With a hasty glance at the altimeter she climbed to a safe height and returned home to make a perfect landing.

"You're doing better every day," the young man praised her as they climbed out. "At this rate you'll soon solo."

"I hope so," grinned Nancy. "I think every girl should learn to fly."

"What do you hear from Ned Nickerson?" the instructor inquired.

"Ned Nickerson?" Nancy tried to act unconcerned, but she blushed becomingly. "Why, I had a letter from him yesterday. He's in South America."

"Miss him, don't you?"

"Yes, I do," Nancy said truthfully. "Ned and I had wonderful times together. He hopes to get home soon. Won't he be surprised when he finds out about my flying?"

"Keep at it, and maybe you'll get your licence before he returns."

Upon reaching home, Nancy sketched an air map of the Heath Castle grounds. The next day she showed it to George and Bess, proposing that they start at once for the estate.

Packing a picnic lunch, the three girls set out in Nancy's car. This time they dressed more appropriately for the trip by wearing riding breeches and stout boots. On the way Nancy explained the latest developments in the mystery.

"Nothing must drive us away from the estate until we've investigated every nook and corner of it," she declared, as the car rocked over the bumpy road. "I'm sure we can find a clue there."

Directly ahead loomed the familiar ivy-covered boundary wall. Nancy parked the automobile beneath a cool tunnel of overhanging tree limbs.

Leaping out, the girls walked to the rusty gate. There they stopped short, staring in dismay. Tacked to the barrier was a freshly painted sign which read:

NO TRESPASSING
UNDER PENALTY OF THE LAW

Chapter IX

THE POINTING FINGER

NANCY and her friends stared at the "No Trespassing" sign, scarcely believing their eyes. It had not been there at the time of their previous visit. Obviously, it was intended to discourage just such persons as themselves from entering the grounds.

"Someone must have seen us here," muttered George in disgust. "Nancy, you were right when you thought you saw a man peering at us from behind the evergreen."

"This puts an end to our exploring," Bess said, disappointed. "We'll have to eat our picnic lunch some other place."

Nancy was not so easily discouraged. She argued that if they were to help Mrs. Fenimore and Joan they would have to do better than Hector Keep had in locating the missing dancer. And no signs were going to keep her from hunting for necessary clues.

"It's most important that we try to find Florianna," she assured her companions. "If the fortune is saved, it probably will mean that Joan and her mother will be provided for."

"They certainly need help," said Bess. "But dare we trespass here?"

"I really have police sanction to do so. Lieutenant Masters urged me to take the case," Nancy replied.

"Then I guess it's all right," said George.

She had walked to the rusty gate to peer between the spikes. The grounds seemed as deserted as ever, but as Nancy and Bess joined her, the girls were startled to hear the sudden barking of dogs.

"Listen!" Nancy exclaimed. An instant later she added, "They're inside the grounds!"

"And coming closer," Bess said uneasily. "They must have heard our car stop here at the gate. Well, that settles it," she declared, almost in relief. "We can't possibly go inside now. We might be chewed to pieces."

She turned as if to go back to the car. George and Nancy lingered by the gate, reluctant to leave. Soon they glimpsed two large black and white hounds through the bushes.

"Ugly-looking brutes," George commented. "Evidently they've been left here to guard the grounds."

Seeing the intruders, the dogs began to bark louder than ever. One of them came to the gate, and with his front paws on the iron bars, growled fiercely at Nancy. Instead of retreating, the girl spoke kindly to him and held out her hand.

"Hello, old fellow," she said soothingly. "When did you come to live here?"

To the amazement of Bess, the animal began to whine in friendly fashion and wag his tail. Reaching a hand through the gate, Nancy patted his head.

"Be careful!" Bess warned her sharply.

To the surprise of the cousins, the other dog had stopped barking and now came forward. Nancy patted his head also and talked to him.

"These dogs aren't vicious!" she said, elated. "Girls, I'm sure we can explore the grounds safely."

"I'm willing to try it if you are," George offered.

Bess was afraid of the dogs and said so. "But I'll come along," she agreed.

"I'll go first," Nancy offered courageously. "If they don't attack me, it will be safe for you two to follow."

George and Bess watched uneasily as their friend climbed the crumbling wall. On the ledge she hesitated a moment. The dogs had set up a loud barking again. Nancy realized that for the animals to be friendly while on the opposite side of an enclosure was one thing; for them to let anyone enter the grounds was another.

"Don't attempt it!" Bess called nervously. "Please!"

Nancy spoke gently but firmly to the hounds. Then, taking a chance, she began to lower herself very gradually. One of the dogs came straight toward the girl. Her heart began to beat wildly, but she showed no outward fear.

"Well, old fellow," she murmured, "do I come in?"

To her relief the animal ceased barking and displayed only a friendly interest in her.

"It's all right," Nancy called to her chums. "Come on over."

She continued to pat the hounds and talk to them as George climbed the wall and leaped down. The dogs did not try to molest her. As soon as Bess's head appeared, however, they began to snarl.

"Don't mind them," Nancy called encouragingly. "They're only testing your nerve."

"They'll tear me to pieces if I jump down there!" Bess was so nervous that she was almost in tears.

"They'll leave you alone if you don't show any fear," Nancy assured her.

It was impossible for the frightened girl to do this. "Go on without me," she said after two vain attempts. "Those dogs just don't like me. I'll wait in the car."

"All right," Nancy agreed. "Don't eat up all the lunch while we're gone!"

She and George set off alone. The dogs remained behind. Soon the girls located the avenue of trees which led past the ruined loggia.

"Here is a path that I'm sure will lead to the castle," Nancy remarked, as they came to a forking trail.

"Maybe," smiled George, "but this sign reads 'To the Fairie Gallerie.'"

"Let's see where it goes anyway," urged Nancy.

They passed a weather-stained statuette in a wall niche; lingered a moment to gaze at a rose garden choked with weeds, then went on to a clearing. Before them rose an artistic structure. The sides were formed of slender twisted stone columns, while sprawling over them was a roof of untrimmed vines, supported by thick stalks. From one end of the shelter hung a rustic sign on which were the words:

> Who enters here may fairies meet,
> With laughter soft they should be greet.

"How pretty," said Nancy dreamily. "Joan Fenimore would adore it here. Incidentally, I'd love to meet a fairy who would reveal the secrets we want to know."

George, surveying the gallery closely, remarked practically, "It looks as if Father Time had taken over here instead of the fairies," adding that the stone columns looked as if they might tumble down any minute.

Nancy stooped to inspect the base of one of the pillars, saying that she was amazed stone could be damaged so greatly by weather.

"George!" she exclaimed suddenly. "Will you look at this?"

"What is it?"

"Someone has deliberately tampered with these columns. See the marks on the stone! They've been weakened— probably with a pickaxe!"

"It does seem that way, Nancy! But why would anyone do that?"

As the girls inspected the other columns, Nancy spoke of the note she had found at the old button factory, and the words "in a wall."

"I'm sure someone is searching in various walls for an article of value," she said. "What it is, I have no idea."

"But why destroy these lovely columns?"

"Maybe the person didn't find what he wants in any of the regular walls, and is now looking in the columns. Oh, if only I had the missing half of the message!"

George was not listening very closely to her friend's words. Instead, she was gazing down the path as if transfixed.

"What do you see?" Nancy asked in a low voice. "Those dogs aren't coming back, are they?"

The other girl shook her head, pointing toward the bushes. Nancy could make out nothing unusual.

"It's an old man!" George whispered. "He's pointing his finger at us!"

Nancy was startled too as she saw the man amid the heavy shrubbery. Her pulse quickened, but she moved toward the figure. Nearing it, she laughed softly.

"Why, it's only a life-sized statue, George!"

Decidedly embarrassed by her mistake, the crestfallen girl went over to inspect the figure.

"That pointing finger may have a special significance," Nancy remarked thoughtfully, noting that the direction indicated was along a path. "Let's follow this and see where it takes us."

The trail had been nearly obliterated by weeds. It twisted in and out among the trees and seemed to lead nowhere. The girls were about to turn back, when Nancy spied the flash of water in filtered sunlight.

It proved to be a large, stagnant pool clogged with water lilies. George went over to inspect it.

"Why do you suppose the statue pointed to this?" she speculated. "It doesn't look like any——"

Her words ended in a little scream, as the soft bank beneath the girl's feet gave way. Before Nancy could make a move to save her friend, she had slipped into the water. It proved not to be deep, but George was soaked.

"Look at me! I'm a mess!" she cried, struggling to her feet. "Now what am I to do?"

Nancy helped her chum scramble up the slippery bank. Gazing about her, she noticed a stone house near by. Apparently it once had been used as a tool shed.

"Go in there and get out of your wet clothes," she advised George. "I'll dry them in the sun for you. It shouldn't take long."

This appeared to be the only solution, so the wet girl disappeared into the stone house. She tossed breeches, blue riding shirt, stockings and shoes through an open window. Nancy spread them on the bank in the sun and started walking around the pond.

On the bank close by, she noticed a whelk shell which evidently had been dislodged from the bottom of the pond by George's fall. At first glance Nancy gave it no thought. Then it occurred to her that it was unusual it should be there.

After a moment's thought, Nancy stripped off shoes and stockings and waded into the shallow water. Dipping her hands into the sand, she discovered that the bottom of the pond was thick with discarded whelk shells.

"This is strange," she mused, "finding these so far from the factory. They couldn't have come from there. And certainly the Heaths wouldn't have eaten this many."

Still trying to figure out a logical answer to the puzzle, she returned to the bank and sat down. Suddenly a thought came to her. Mehearty had said that whelks were used in making fine dyes. Walter Heath had spent much of his time on scientific experiments. Was it not reasonable to suppose that the estate owner had been using whelks to perfect some kind of dye for use at the button factory?

"Hey, why so pensive?" George called, interrupting Nancy's thoughts. "See if my clothes are dry, will you?"

Nancy obediently arose and felt of George's garments. "Not yet," she reported.

"I'm getting hungry," complained George. "And Bess will be having a fit if we don't get back."

In this she was right. Hungry herself, and tired of waiting, Bess was fuming in Nancy's concealed car. As the sun climbed high overhead and the others failed to return, the girl became annoyed.

"Guess they've forgotten me," she thought.

To add to her irritation, the hounds came dashing back to the gate when she walked over to look through it. Seeing her, they bayed savagely.

"Just wait until I see George and Nancy!" Bess stormed. "I'll——"

Just then she heard a car coming up the road. Bess barely had time to hide herself in the bushes before it swung around the bend. She was glad that she had hidden herself, for she was sure from Nancy's description that the driver was none other than Hector Keep. He was alone.

To the girl's dismay he got out and walked all around, thereby spotting Nancy's car. The man muttered something that Bess could not hear. Finally he went to the double gate and unlocked it.

"He's going to drive into the grounds!" Bess told herself. "Nancy and George will be caught trespassing! Oh, I must warn them!"

Fairly beside herself with anxiety, the girl did not know what to do. Hector Keep still had his back turned toward her. The sedan, its engine running, was not ten feet away.

There was no time to think or plan. Impulsively, Bess darted to the car. Climbing into the back part, she crouched on the floor.

Hector Keep returned to the automobile. Unaware of his passenger, he drove through the gates into the estate grounds.

Chapter X

NANCY EXPLORES

"GEORGE, would you mind if I do a little exploring?" Nancy asked. "I'll be back by the time your clothes are dry."

"Don't you dare leave me in the lurch!" the other girl warned her.

Nancy smiled. "I'm not going far. But I've just found a lot of whelk shells, and I think they may indicate something important. Perhaps some bottles of dye from them are hidden near by."

She moved off, looking about carefully for any possible storage space: a small building, a hidden enclosure. None appeared, and in her search Nancy wandered farther than she had intended.

"What's that?" she wondered when she became aware of a low rumble which seemed to shake the earth.

She stood still and waited, but there was no further sound. In the distance a cloud of white, powdery dust caught her attention.

"Another explosion!" she murmured excitedly. "Maybe that's what happened yesterday when I was in the plane and thought I saw smoke down here!"

Cautiously she went toward the scene, but her path was blocked by a high briar hedge over which she could not climb without scratching herself severely. Following the hedge for some distance to find an opening, Nancy was startled to hear the sound of an automobile.

"Someone must have driven into the estate grounds!"

The sound drew nearer. Deciding to find out who the newcomer was, Nancy plunged through the woodland. She reached a weed-grown clearing just as Hector Keep drove up and stopped.

Nancy drew back quickly into the shelter of the protecting bushes. The man did not see her. Parking his car under a gnarled maple, he got out and set off on foot.

"I'll follow him," the girl thought impulsively.

Hector Keep walked so fast that Nancy could scarcely keep him in sight. The lawyer seemed thoroughly acquainted with the many trails, for he never hesitated when he came to a turn.

Before long the man vanished from view. When Nancy came to a fork in the path, she wondered which way he had gone. Fearful lest she lose track of him entirely, she pressed her ear to the ground and very faintly could make out a steady beat on the right fork. Thus guided, she hastened on.

Presently this trail branched off in three directions. Again Nancy was baffled. When she flattened herself on the ground this time she could hear no sound.

"I've lost him!" she thought in dismay.

Choosing a path at random, she went on doggedly. For the moment she was so intent on her sleuthing that she completely forgot about George and Bess.

Meanwhile Bess, still hidden in Hector Keep's car, was wondering what to do. Though Nancy had been near by, she had not seen her. Deciding she had better find her cousin and her chum, Bess cautiously climbed from the automobile and started up the trail the lawyer had taken.

Bess had not gone far before she became alarmed. The dogs had begun to bark. They were coming closer to her each moment.

"They've picked up my scent!" the girl thought in terror.

The hounds bounded into view, and Bess was thrown into a panic. She shinned up a tree, hoping the dogs would pass by, but instead they took up a vigil at the base of the trunk.

Back at the tool house, George Fayne had grown tired of waiting for Nancy to return. From the window she could see her clothes on the sunny bank of the pond. They seemed to be dry.

"I can't wait another minute!" she thought impatiently. "I'll go and get them myself!"

George went to the door of the tool house and there stopped short. A tousy-haired boy in faded overalls had emerged from among the trees. He appeared to be eleven or twelve years old.

Ducking out of sight behind the door, the girl watched the lad. To her consternation he wandered toward the pond. Seeing the clothes, he suddenly snatched them up and hurried off.

"Hey, you! Those are mine!" George cried angrily from the window.

The boy did not hear her; or if he did, he paid no attention.

"Good night!" George cried out in despair. "Now what'll I do? Nancy's done a disappearing act, and I'm stranded here without any clothes!"

Unaware of the difficulties of her two chums, Nancy was intent upon another subject. The trail she had chosen had not led her to Hector Keep, but it had brought her to Heath Castle. She could not resist the temptation to see the wonderful building at close range, for its beauty, even at a distance, awed her.

It was constructed of massive grey stone covered in large part by ivy. The roof line was broken by several turrets, a large one at each end of the great residence, with smaller ones in between.

"It's a perfect copy of an old English castle," Nancy decided, "only smaller. Oh, if Mrs. Fenimore and Joan could only come here and get away from that dingy house they live in and that dreadful Jeddy Hooker!"

Her thoughts were interrupted by a faraway, plaintive cry. At first she thought it was the same sound which had frightened Bess on the girls' previous visit to the estate. Now she wondered. When the sound was repeated, it seemed more human.

A wild thought crossed Nancy's mind. Was someone in

the castle in distress? Perhaps Florianna *was* being held a prisoner in one of the tower rooms!

"Oh, I must get inside!" she determined. "If someone is in need of help——"

The girl began to circle the castle walls, reflecting as she looked at their stateliness that it was a pity they had to stand in the midst of a ruined garden. A massive side door of the big house stood ajar. Nancy wondered whether Hector Keep had opened it. She hesitated to trespass, then decided if someone were in trouble, it was her duty to aid the person. Without further ado she slipped into the dwelling.

The girl found herself in a long corridor which twisted and turned crazily. Large rooms lined with beautiful, panelled wood opened from it. Many of these rooms were empty, others contained a few pieces of fine old mahogany furniture. At a glance, it was apparent to Nancy that nearly everything of value had been removed from the place.

"Odd," she mused. "I thought the castle was left to Florianna intact."

The inside wooden shutters in the gloomy rooms were closed, giving the few sheet-draped chairs a ghostly appearance. The unexpected sight of herself in a long mirror gave Nancy a momentary fright. At the same time she heard the plaintive cry again. It seemed to come from upstairs.

Quickly Nancy found steps leading to the second story. A search of the rooms there, including all of the many closets, revealed nothing.

"The only places left are the towers," the girl decided. "But how do I get into them?"

Try as she might, she could locate no entrance to any of the turrets. Then, chancing to glance from a window, she realized that the castle was built around a hollow square, which proved to be another tangled garden. Nancy figured that some of the bedrooms actually were the smaller turrets. The high towers no doubt were separate, with doors to them opening from the courtyard garden.

"How like olden times to imprison someone in a tower!"

she thought, as she heard the plaintive cry again and hurried down the stairway to hunt for an exit to the inner garden.

The door to it lay hidden in the shadows of the corridor, so Nancy did not locate it at once. When she did, she quickly tripped the bolt so she would not lock herself out, and stepped into the sunshine.

Glancing around, the young detective discovered her guess had been right. There were entrance doors to the two high, round towers. As she opened the first one, she held her breath, wondering what lay beyond.

What Nancy actually saw was disappointing. Apparently the tower had been built for architectural purposes only. The room in which the girl stood had a low ceiling and contained nothing. Its only interest lay in the fact that the circular stone wall appeared to have been chipped and damaged.

"Even the castle hasn't escaped investigation by that fellow who's hunting for the secret," Nancy thought.

She turned her attention to the other tower, glad that the massive door to it was not locked. Here a different sight met the girl's eyes, and again she faintly heard the plaintive cry.

"Maybe the person in trouble is in here!" she reflected.

The stone tower was hollow and only dimly lighted by a window high up. A circular iron stairway led to a half balcony at the top. Nancy looked around on the ground floor but saw nothing. As speedily as possible she ascended the steps and found a little door at the head of them. Cautiously she pushed on it and peeked beyond.

Would she find anyone there?

As her eyes became accustomed to the sombre light, she saw that there was nothing in the tiny room, nor on the open parapet beyond it. In disappointment Nancy leaned on the wide rail.

"All this work, just to get a view," she thought ruefully. "But at least it gives me a better idea of the place than I got from the plane. That cry, though——"

Suddenly her attention was drawn to a running figure in the distance far below her. Nancy strained her eyes to see who it was.

"Oh, my goodness!" she exclaimed with a fearful pang of conscience.

Beyond a boundary wall of the estate, a boy was crossing the beach toward a boat. And behind him, trailing in the sand, were George's hiking clothes!

Chapter XI

LOCKED IN THE TOWER

As Nancy watched from the tower balcony, the boy accidentally dropped one of the garments on the grassy sand by the river bank.

"George's riding pants!" the girl thought in dismay.

Nancy was too far away to call to the boy. She saw him dart to the water's edge, jump into a boat, and row away.

"I never should have left George alone at the tool house," she blamed herself.

Realizing that she must do something at once to help her friend, Nancy retraced her steps through the balcony to the stairway, ran down the steps, and raced to the courtyard door.

When she tried to pull it open, it would not budge. She yanked and yanked. Finally the disturbing realization came to her that someone had locked it.

She was a prisoner in the tower!

"Oh, I must get out!" she told herself.

Nancy refused to allow herself to become panicky. Surely there must be some way to get out! Returning to the open parapet, she looked about her.

It was a forty-foot drop to the ground, and far too dangerous for her to attempt. Thoroughly discouraged, the girl went down to try the locked door again. As she twisted the knob, Nancy thought she heard the sound of voices. Her heart leaped! Two men were just outside. They were coming nearer.

"We'll get caught, I tell you!" one was arguing in a loud voice. "And if we are, the old man'll say he never saw us before!"

"Oh, quit your worrying," the other growled. "Just leave the brain work on this job to me. We'll find that clue yet. It's somewhere in one of the walls on the estate."

"Yeah? Which wall?" the first man asked sarcastically. "The place is full of 'em! Anyhow, I'm satisfied with what we've found already and kept for ourselves!"

"When he sees all the walls we've blasted, he can't deny we did a pretty thorough job for him!" the other snickered.

The voices faded out, and Nancy guessed that the two speakers had moved away. Who were the men? The voice of one was entirely unfamiliar. Though she could not be sure, she thought that the other man might be the one whose motorboat had crashed into her own. Though she had not heard him speak at the time of the accident, this man's voice was certainly that of the person she had suspected and spoken to near the dock. Nancy was sure he was the one for whom she was looking, even though he had denied it.

"Well, that proves a few of my theories!" the girl thought grimly. "The walls of Heath Castle and the gardens have been damaged deliberately, and on orders from someone who wants to find a clue! Evidently those men have located something of interest, too. It could be the missing half of the note I picked up; or it could be something connected with Walter Heath's experiments. Or it could very well concern Florianna."

Hoping to catch a glimpse of the men, the girl returned to the parapet and watched eagerly. She did not see them, but a moment later she heard them whistling and calling to the dogs. Then all became quiet again.

"They've gone!" Nancy thought uneasily. "Maybe I

should have let them know I'm here when I had the chance. But no, they're not honest, and they probably would have ruined all my plans. I'll get out somehow!"

The girl was in a predicament, nevertheless. George, stranded without clothes at the tool house, could not help her. Bess, so far as she knew, was waiting in the parked car outside the castle gates.

Nancy roved restlessly about the ground floor of the tower, searching vainly for an exit. To add to her dismay, she was very hungry. Looking at her watch for the first time, the imprisoned girl was amazed to discover that it was after two o'clock.

"If I ever do get out of here, George and Bess will skin me alive!" she thought with a guilty smile.

But if she had only known! Bess Marvin at that moment was frantically trying to save her own skin. She was perched in a tree a considerable distance from the castle. Surrounded by watchful dogs, she was afraid to descend for fear they might tear her to pieces.

In the midst of a state bordering on tears, she was startled to hear whistling. The dogs heard the sound, too. They pricked up their ears, then went racing away.

"Thank goodness!" Bess gasped, sliding down from her leafy prison.

So much time had elapsed that she decided it would do no good to try to find Nancy and George. Had they not encountered Hector Keep already, they surely would have returned to the parked car.

"I'll go back there," Bess concluded. "But which way did I come?" she wondered.

Hopelessly confused, she started off, unwittingly taking a trail leading toward the river. After a long walk Bess found her way blocked by a crumbling wall. One of the stones had fallen out, creating a perfect peephole. The girl peered through it, hoping to see the road. Instead, she saw the river stretching out below her. On the nearby beach lay a pair of riding breeches.

"George's clothes!" she identified them instantly.

There was no sign of either George or Nancy. Bess could not believe that her chums had gone for a swim.

"My cousin must be in trouble!" she concluded in panic.

Bess tried to climb the wall, but the stones crumbled beneath her fingers. Once she nearly made it, only to lose her hold and fall.

"I'll go back to the car," she decided at last. "If Nancy and George aren't there, then the only thing to do is go to River Heights for help."

Stumbling through the tall grass, the girl came to a path. By this time she was so beside herself with anxiety she failed to observe that it had been trampled recently.

The trail, Bess soon discovered, did not lead toward the main gate. Instead, she came to a crescent-shaped pond covered thickly with water lilies.

"Oh, where am I?" she asked herself desperately.

A stiff breeze was stirring the trees, rustling the leaves and rubbing the branches together. A dead limb came tumbling down. Bess leaped aside, and as she did so, she thought she heard someone call her name.

"It was just my imagination," she told herself sternly. "I must be hearing things."

Then the cry came again. "Bess! Bess!"

The girl whirled around. She could see no one. A few yards away stood a stone tool house, its window hidden by overhanging tree branches.

"Bess!" the voice shouted impatiently. "Over here! In the tool house!"

This time Bess could not doubt but that it was her cousin who had called her. Hastening to the little building, she looked inside.

"I thought you never would pay attention to me!" George regarded her accusingly. "I've been stranded here for hours! Just wait until I get my hands on Nancy Drew!"

"George, where are your clothes?" Bess gasped in astonishment.

"Where are they indeed? I fell into the pond and had to take off my clothes. Nancy put them on the bank to dry.

Then she went to do some exploring. A boy came along and ran away with my things!"

"How terrible! What became of Nancy?"

"I wish I knew." George's sense of resentment vanished. It was replaced by a feeling of anxiety. "She's been gone a long while."

"Perhaps she went back to the car."

"That's possible, though it's not like Nancy to desert anyone. She knew I'd be waiting here for her."

"We must hunt for her right away, George. Hector Keep is somewhere on the grounds!"

"Hector Keep here?" George echoed in alarm. "Oh, we must find Nancy and get away before he sees us. But how can I go anywhere this way?"

Bess slipped off the raincoat she was wearing.

"Take this," she offered. "I don't need it."

George put it on, and was relieved to find her shoes still lying near the bank of the pond. Bess told her that she had seen the riding breeches down on the beach by the river.

"Let them stay there for the time being," George decided. "Our first job is to find Nancy."

The girls waited no longer. Convinced that their chum was not coming, they set off in search of her.

"Let's go back to the car first," George proposed. "She may be waiting there."

Without meeting anyone, and without being molested by the dogs, the cousins finally got to the front wall and climbed over. Nancy was not in the automobile.

"Let's drive to town and bring help," Bess said nervously.

"Drive, did you say? Nancy has the keys to the car."

"Oh, I'd forgotten! Well, we are in a nice mess!"

"We'll have to find Nancy; that's all there is to it. She must be somewhere inside the estate grounds."

Fortifying themselves with sandwiches from the lunch they had brought, the girls started to scale the wall again. On the ledge, they hesitated. The dogs had come back and now began to growl menacingly.

"Maybe if we feed them——" George suggested.

She hopped down and got two sandwiches from the car. At sight of the food the hounds became friendly, but the instant they had gobbled it up, they lay on the ground, panting and waiting. Again and again George tried to descend, but each time the dogs rose menacingly.

Bess would not even try. "It's no use," she sighed. "We may as well wait in the car."

This did not please George at all; but try as she might, she could not figure out how to get inside the grounds. The dogs showed no inclination to leave. Whenever George went near the wall, they started barking.

An hour elapsed, and still another. The afternoon sun slipped lower behind the trees, and long shadows darkened the woodland road. Only then did the girls conclude that Nancy must be in serious trouble. Otherwise, she would have returned by this time.

"We can't sit here and wait another instant!" George cried, leaping from the car. "Bess, we must do something right away!"

Bess agreed. "I'll go for help," she said.

Chapter XII

THE TRAP DOOR

FOR hours, Nancy had refused to acknowledge that there was no means of escape from the tower. She had pried at the door lock with a nail file from her bag. She had tried to break the wooden panels by sheer force, but their strength had defied her.

Now she wandered aimlessly about the circular room. She had been without food and water so many hours, she began to feel faint. Twice she seriously considered swinging herself over the parapet and making the long drop to the ground, but gave up the idea as foolhardy.

"I'd be certain to break some bones if I did that," she reasoned.

As time dragged by, Nancy grew more and more desperate. She wondered what had become of George. The poor girl! And Bess. What of her? With a feeling of utter dismay Nancy realized that she had the car keys with her. She certainly had gotten herself and her friends into a dreadful muddle.

Nancy sank down on the bottom step of the winding iron staircase to try to figure things out. She stared straight ahead of her.

"This is the worst trap I've ever been in!" she decided unhappily.

Suddenly the distraught girl became aware of something on the floor in front of her. A tiny crack neatly outlined a rectangular space about three feet square.

"Speaking of traps!" Nancy muttered. "Maybe this is a trap door! A chance to escape!"

Quickly dropping to her hands and knees, she inspected the crack. Obviously, it marked the outline of an opening, but there was no ring or handle with which to pull up the trap door.

Nancy pried at it first with her fingers and then with her nail file. The slender bit of steel snapped in her hands.

"Oh, how can I get it open?" she fumed, looking around for something heavier with which to lift it.

Not a single object was in the tower. After an hour Nancy discarded the possibility of this means of escape. The room grew stuffy to her; or was it because she felt almost ill from lack of nourishment? Her tongue parched and her head aching, she slowly climbed the stairs and went out on the parapet to get some fresh air.

The sky became overcast. In a short time it was almost dark. Except for the occasional hoot of an owl and the intermittent croaking of frogs, there was not a sound. Then suddenly Nancy became aware of approaching footsteps.

Her first impulse was to shout to make her whereabouts known, as she thought someone had come to rescue her. But intuition warned her to remain silent.

Springing to her feet, she looked over the parapet. A man she was sure was a stranger to her was unlocking the door far below her. He snapped on a flashlight and entered the tower.

Nancy's heart pounded. Should she walk boldly down the stairs and try to bluff her way out?

"No, I mustn't do that," she decided. "If something sinister is going on at Heath Castle, this man probably is involved."

She concluded that should he find her, all her chances to help Mrs. Fenimore and Joan would be ruined.

"Maybe I can get out of here while the man is busy," the girl thought hopefully. "He may have opened that trap door and gone down below."

Nancy tiptoed across the little balcony room. Fortunately she did not reach the doorway, for at that instant a light flashed through the opening. It missed revealing her presence by a fraction of an inch.

As Nancy shrank into the shadows, the man began to ascend the iron staircase. With sinking heart the trapped girl stepped back of the door and pressed herself against the wall.

The intruder went directly to the parapet. As Nancy peeked out, he began to move his light slowly up and down as if he were signalling. In the backward reflection of the rays which dimly revealed his face, Nancy knew that she had never seen this cruel-looking person before.

Though she longed to watch what he was doing, she dared not tarry. This was her opportunity to escape! Tiptoeing around the door, she started down the stairway. On the third step from the bottom she stumbled. To her oversensitive ears the noise was loud and grating. Had the stranger heard her?

Quick as lightning she darted down the rest of the steps and reached the courtyard garden in safety. Hurrying to the arched doorway, the girl was relieved to find it was still unlocked.

She groped her way along the dark corridor in the castle. A moment later her knee bumped into a piece of furniture, striking it so hard that she nearly cried out in pain.

Another precious ten minutes was lost as she carefully felt along the dark walls for a door to the grounds. At last her efforts were rewarded. With a deep sigh of relief, she rushed into the open.

"What an adventure!" Nancy shuddered. "Now if only I can find George and Bess!"

By no means were the girl's troubles at an end. She hoped that in the dusky light she would be able to find her way out. She knew the direction toward the main gate, but with weed-grown paths, treacherous rocks, and roaming dogs, she would have to be very cautious. It was fully an hour before Nancy saw the vague outline of a wall ahead of her.

"I hope it's the one near my car," she said to herself. "Oh——"

Something was moving through the bushes. In an instant the stillness was broken by the sharp barking of dogs.

"Can I trust them?" Nancy wondered. "They may not be friendly after dark!"

She made a leap for the crumbling wall and scrambled up, reaching the top just as the two hounds arrived. The Drew girl dropped breathlessly to the other side and got her bearings.

"The car must be up there a short way," she concluded, starting off.

Five minutes later she came to the automobile. To her amazement and delight George was huddled in a raincoat on the back seat. She was half asleep.

"George!"

The girl sat bolt upright, and gave a little scream.

"It's Nancy!"

"Oh, you scared me nearly out of my wits."

"Sorry. Where's Bess?"

"Gone to get your father. Oh, Nancy, what in the world happened to you?"

"Plenty! But first, tell me, how long ago did Bess leave? Would it be best for us to wait?"

"She went hours ago, but it's a long walk to a bus or a phone. Somebody ought to be here any minute, though, it seems to me."

The two girls exchanged stories. George told how she and Bess had become almost frantic over Nancy's disappearance. Fearing she might be in Hector Keep's clutches, Bess had offered to summon Mr. Drew.

"After Bess left, I heard a noise in the grounds," George related, "so I hid in the bushes near the gate. Mr. Keep drove out. While he was locking the gate, I peeked in his car to see if you were there. I really expected you to be lying on the floor, bound hand and foot!"

"I was a prisoner, all right, but not tied up," Nancy smiled—she could smile now. "Then what happened?"

"Mr. Keep went straight to your car."

"He must have seen it when he came, too," Nancy groaned. "And I thought I had hidden it well. Now all he has to do is look up the licence number and he'll know who was here."

"It's a shame," said George. "And it's too bad about my clothes. I didn't tell you what happened to them."

"I know. While I was looking out of the tower, a boy took them away in a rowboat. Who was he, do you know?"

"I never saw him before. He was about twelve years old. But I'd like to wring his neck, the little thief! My best shirt! Why, Nancy, that shirt came from the Bon Ton and I paid a mint of money for it!"

"If we find Florianna and the Heath money is turned over to her, maybe she'll buy you a new one," teased Nancy. Then, suddenly making a discovery, she added, "Say, there isn't any food left."

"No, Bess and I ate every scrap of the lunch. Nancy, that man in the tower. Where do you suppose he came from? No car drove in here."

"He must have come up the river," the Drew girl replied. "Unless he lives on the place," she added as an afterthought.

A moving path of light suddenly cut the darkness. An automobile! Was Carson Drew driving it, or was Hector Keep returning?

With bated breaths the two girls waited, wondering if they should hide or stand their ground. George, weary of the whole thing, favoured the latter, but Nancy felt this move unwise, so together they scrambled out of sight.

The car stopped. Bess Marvin alighted. "Why, George is gone!" she wailed.

"No, she isn't," her cousin spoke up, walking forward. "We were just being careful."

"We?"

"Nancy is here."

Nancy herself was running to the side of the car from which her father had stepped. In an instant she was in his arms.

"Why, Dad, you're trembling!" she said.

"Nancy, Nancy, I'm so glad to see you. You gave me such a fright. Where——"

"Oh, I'm dreadfully sorry I made such a mess of things," his daughter apologized. "But maybe you'll forgive me when I tell you what happened."

"Tell me about it on the way home. Bess can drive your car as far as her house, then you take it the rest of the way."

On the return to River Heights Mr. Drew listened without comment, until Nancy had concluded. Her closing sentence made him wrinkle his forehead.

"I'm convinced," said Nancy, "that something sinister is going on at Heath Castle and in the gardens. The walls there aren't crumbling from age, Dad—they're being tampered with for some purpose!"

"I agree it looks mighty suspicious," said Mr. Drew. "And Hector Keep may be involved. But suppose you put the whole case out of your mind for a while, at least until you've had a square meal!"

Upon reaching the Drew residence, Nancy made a beeline for the refrigerator. Hannah Gruen, who had been nearly beside herself with worry, could not understand Nancy's attitude. But upon hearing that nothing worse than hunger was the matter with the girl, the housekeeper smiled.

"I guess that's youth for you," she murmured. Then aloud she added, "You poor child. I'll fix you a warm supper right away."

The woman hastened to prepare a meal. Too hungry to wait for the food to cook, Nancy helped herself to a glass of milk and a few cookies. As she ate and drank, she related the highlights of her adventure to the housekeeper.

"Oh, Nancy," Mrs. Gruen sighed, "your love of mystery will yet prove your undoing! You must be more careful."

"I'm not sure that you should return to Heath Castle," said Mr. Drew, coming into the kitchen.

Nancy nearly spilled her glass of milk. "Oh, Dad!" she protested.

"Why not forget the whole affair for a few days?"

"But time is so short——"

"As it happens, I'm going away on a little trip, Nancy. I thought you might enjoy coming along."

"Oh, Dad, you know I would at any other time."

"I plan to go by car, and must interview several persons along the way regarding a legal case."

"Where is the place?" Nancy inquired, still without much interest.

"Hampton."

Nancy shook her head. "If you'll excuse me, Dad, I believe I'd rather stay here and try to solve the mystery about Florianna."

"I'm sorry," Mr. Drew said, his eyes twinkling. "I thought Hampton might prove of interest to you, especially since it was the town where Florianna Johnson last was seen."

Nancy could scarcely believe her ears. "Say that again, Dad!" she cried.

"I was talking with Doctor Gibson in Henryville today," Mr. Drew revealed. "He looked after Florianna, you know;

in fact, he advised her to take the trip from which she never returned."

"Tell me more!"

"There's not much to tell. Florianna was thin and run down, so the doctor advised her to take a vacation. He suggested she slip off to a quiet place without telling anyone where she was going."

"Did the doctor know where she went?"

"No, but her sister Vera Fenimore told him she had seen a railroad ticket in Florianna's purse. The destination was Hampton."

"Oh, Dad, I give in," Nancy stated, trying not to appear too excited. "I'll go with you!"

"I rather thought you would," laughed Mr. Drew.

"When do we leave?"

"Tomorrow morning. Better pack your suitcase tonight."

Chapter XIII

IN SEARCH OF CLUES

NANCY was up early the next morning. She had been too weary the night before to attempt any packing, so she did it now and then skipped downstairs. When she appeared in the kitchen, Hannah Gruen said cheerily:

"Good morning. The mail came a few minutes ago. There's a letter I think you'll want to see. It's on the living room table."

Nancy ran to get it. A glance at the handwriting caused her pulses to quicken. The letter was from Ned Nickerson!

Hurrying to a window seat, Nancy eagerly opened the envelope. She admired Ned Nickerson, and had missed him since he had gone to South America.

"I can't say I'm having a good time," Ned wrote, "but I'm doing some interesting work. I miss you and all the fun we had together. Remember those mysteries we used to solve? You did most of the work and I went along for company. I'm willing to bet that you're head over heels in a mystery this very minute. Right?"

"Right you are, Ned!" Nancy laughed happily as she tucked the missive away for another reading later on. "How I wish Ned were here to help me!"

Mr. Drew came downstairs and said they ought to eat at once and be off. Nancy hoped they might stop for a few minutes at Mrs. Fenimore's to gather any additional information the woman might have about her sister.

"We practically go past her house," she said.

"All right, we'll drop in for a few minutes," the lawyer agreed reluctantly. "But let's make it snappy. I must be in Hampton before noon."

Mrs. Fenimore was delighted to see Nancy again. When the girl presented her father, the woman expressed pleasure that she had brought him with her.

"We're en route to Hampton," Mr. Drew explained, coming straight to the point. "Nancy thought that you might be able to tell us a little more about your sister's disappearance. We understand that you believe your sister went to Hampton."

"Why, yes," the invalid replied. "I don't actually know that Florianna went there, but I did see a ticket to Hampton which she had bought."

"I've given your sister's strange disappearance considerable thought," Mr. Drew confessed. "It strikes me that she must have had a definite reason for abandoning her career."

"Oh, Florianna loved her work!" Mrs. Fenimore protested. "Of course, she was tired and run down, but a few weeks' rest should have put her in good health again."

"We know that after leaving here, Florianna never danced again. Now, if she still lives, she must have earned a living by some means. Did she have any special aptitude for anything except dancing? Could she teach music, for example?" the lawyer asked.

Mrs. Fenimore shook her head. "Florianna was interested

in nothing except dancing. Oh, yes, I might add she loved gardening. My sister was very fond of flowers and liked to grow them." The invalid sighed as she added, "In that respect, Joan takes after her aunt."

"Is Joan at school?" Nancy asked.

"Yes," replied Mrs. Fenimore. "The child worries me," she said with deep concern. "Lieutenant Masters had to come here yesterday to get a plant that had been taken from the park. Oh, I've reprimanded Joan for doing such things, but it does no good."

"I suppose Lieutenant Masters talked to Joan about it?" Mr. Drew inquired.

"Yes. She insisted that she had not taken the plant, that Jeddy Hooker had given it to her. Lieutenant Masters then went next door to speak to Jeddy."

This report about Joan upset Nancy. The child had promised her that she would not play with the boy, but apparently she had done so.

"I'm sure your daughter is telling the truth," she remarked, but in her own heart she was not so certain of this. As soon as she should have time, she must talk it over with Lieutenant Masters.

Since Mrs. Fenimore had told everything she knew regarding her long-missing sister, Nancy and Mr. Drew bade her good-bye and left the house.

"I have a theory I didn't mention," the lawyer commented as he led the way to the car. "Florianna may have married after she left home. In that event, she would have had some means of support."

"But, Dad, wouldn't she have notified Mrs. Fenimore of such a marriage? She had no apparent reason for keeping her whereabouts a secret."

"Quite true. Well, perhaps we'll run into a few clues at Hampton."

Mr. Drew entered the parked car. Nancy was about to follow when she observed a thin, sharp-faced woman with unkempt hair hanging out clothes in the yard adjoining the Fenimore cottage.

"That must be Jeddy Hooker's mother," she told herself. Nancy's attention centred not upon the woman, but on the clothing she was pinning to the line. A blue riding shirt looked strangely familiar to her.

"If that isn't George's stolen shirt, then it's one just like it!" she told herself grimly.

Acting impulsively, Nancy walked over to the yard. The woman saw her coming and eyed her suspiciously.

"Is Jeddy here?" the girl inquired, her manner pleasant.

"No, he ain't," the woman snapped. "He's at school, same as every day."

Working up to the subject, Nancy asked her if Jeddy liked to go boating on the river.

"All boys play around the water," Mrs. Hooker answered. Then, as if fearful she had revealed too much, she added, "Jeddy ain't been on the river lately, though."

Nancy was convinced the woman was not telling the truth. She was certain, too, that the shirt was the same one she herself had hung on a tree limb to dry at Heath Castle. It was a very expensive make; one not likely to have been purchased by Mrs. Hooker. At that instant a gust of wind came and turned the garment in such a way that the label on it became visible. It said *Bon Ton*.

"That's a good-looking riding shirt," Nancy commented, trying not to show her excitement. "Do you ride?"

The woman ignored the question. "Ain't I got a right to have nice things, same as other folks?" she demanded defiantly.

"Why, certainly," Nancy answered in an even tone.

"You must be another one of those snoopy policewomen! Well, I won't talk to you!" snapped the woman.

Snatching the shirt from the line, Mrs. Hooker hurried into the house and slammed the door.

Returning to the car, Nancy related the conversation to her father. Though he agreed with his daughter that her suspicion was justified, he thought her method of approach hardly warranted a confession from Mrs. Hooker.

"You didn't expect the woman to break down and admit

her own son's theft, did you, Nancy? Now you have put her on her guard."

"I never thought of that, Dad," Nancy agreed. "I might have had better luck if I had talked to Jeddy."

Mr. Drew had expected to reach their destination by noon, and had not counted on a long detour which extended the trip many miles. It was well toward three o'clock in the afternoon when he and Nancy arrived at Hampton's one and only hotel.

"Not much time left for work," the lawyer remarked, after the bags had been put into their suite. "But we can get in a little investigating before dinnertime. Meet you here at six, Nancy. Good luck!"

The young detective started off. She decided to make her first call at the railroad station to which Florianna was supposed to have come. The agent in charge dashed Nancy's hopes by telling her he was a new man on the job. The former agent had moved to California two years before.

Nancy refused to be discouraged. Going outside, she interviewed half a dozen elderly taxi drivers whose cabs regularly provided service to and from the station. Not one of the men had driven a cab ten years before, and therefore could give no information regarding the well-known dancer.

"If Florianna came to this town, it seems likely that someone would have recognized her," Nancy reflected. "I'll not give up yet."

At the town hall, where all records were kept, she had no better luck, and by five-thirty she was back at the hotel.

"May I look at your old registers?" she requested the clerk in charge, telling him why she wanted them.

Obligingly he brought out one containing the names of guests who has stayed at the hotel ten years before. Florianna's name was not among them; nor had anyone by the name of Flossie Johnson signed. If the dancer ever had registered there, it had been under an assumed name.

"Have you tried the tourist homes?" the clerk suggested, attempting to be helpful. "We have a dozen of them here— several were in business ten years ago."

"Thank you, that's a good suggestion," Nancy smiled.

The following morning she went to the office of the Board of Health, where she obtained a list of all guest houses in operation at the time of Florianna's disappearance. With renewed hope, she set out to interview the owners of the establishments still operating. The experience was not entirely pleasant, for upon one occasion a woman, finding the girl did not want a room, slammed the door in her face! And nowhere did she obtain the desired information.

"It's just no use," Nancy thought, ringing the doorbell of the last house on her list. "I'm at the end of my rope."

There was a delay before anyone came to open the door of the little cottage. Finally a kindly, grey-haired woman appeared.

"If you're looking for a room, I'm afraid I'll have to disappoint you," she said before the girl could speak. "A young lady rented my only vacant one not ten minutes ago."

"I'm not looking for a room," Nancy explained with a smile. "I came to ask about someone who may have stayed with you some years back."

"I'll be happy to help you if I can."

Nancy told her listener that she was trying to locate a woman who had come to the town several years ago.

"You say the young woman's name was Florianna Johnson?" inquired the woman.

"That was her stage name. She also was known as Flossie Johnson."

Nancy waited, fully expecting her hopes to be dashed again. Instead, the owner of the tourist house smiled and pushed open the screen door.

"Come in," she invited cordially. "I think I can help you."

Chapter XIV

ENCOURAGING INFORMATION

"I am Mrs. Delbert," the owner of the tourist home told Nancy. She led the girl into a parlour stuffy with old-fashioned plush furniture. "You are——?"

"Nancy Drew. I'm a stranger here in Hampton."

"Hardly a stranger by name," corrected the old lady. "Frequently I've seen stories in the newspapers about your fine detective work. I never thought I'd have the pleasure of actually meeting you."

Nancy flushed at the compliment. Sensing the girl's embarrassment, Mrs. Delbert said quickly:

"You are in a hurry, I know, so I'll tell you what I can about Florianna. She came here ten years ago this month and rented my front room for one night."

"She told you her name?"

"Not at first. She just said 'Miss Johnson.' The first night she was here she was taken ill. I nursed her for three days."

"Was the illness serious?" Nancy asked quickly.

"No. She seemed more exhausted than anything. The young woman was run down and thin as a rail. I took care of her, and at the end of three days she was strong enough to leave."

Nancy asked the old lady to describe Miss Johnson.

"I can show you her picture," Mrs. Delbert volunteered. From a table drawer she produced a photograph which she placed in the girl's hand. "After Miss Johnson left, I found this lying on the dresser in her room. Read what she wrote on it."

In appreciation
To Mrs. Delbert from Florianna

"This is Florianna's picture and handwriting," Nancy said, identifying it instantly from a similar one in Mrs.

Fenimore's possession. "Do you know where the young woman went after she left here?"

"Miss Johnson said she might stay a few weeks on a farm near Plainville."

"She didn't give you the address?"

"No." After a pause she added, "I've always been sorry I never went later on to see her dance, but I rarely get away from here."

"So far as anyone knows, Florianna gave up her dancing," Nancy explained. "She disappeared ten years ago."

Mrs. Delbert's eyes opened wide. "How dreadful! And you are trying to find her? Oh, I hope you do. She was such a lovely person."

"Is Plainville far from here?" Nancy inquired. "I'll try that place next."

"About thirty miles. There's no train service from here to Plainville. And that was a funny thing, too. When Florianna left here, she directed the taxi driver to take her to the railroad station. But she couldn't have gone to Plainville by train, for there is none."

"Maybe she didn't realize that at the time," Nancy suggested, "and later went by some other route."

Thanking the old lady for her assistance, Nancy hastened to the Hampton Hotel. At luncheon she repeated to her father what she had learned.

"You've done well, Nancy," he praised her. "You've picked up a far better clue than I expected you would."

"Then, as my reward, will you take me to Plainville?"

"I expected that request," Mr. Drew chuckled. "Yes, we'll go on if you wish. My work here is finished, so I'll have the time to spare."

The drive to Plainville was a pleasant one over rolling hills. Several towns lay along the way. At a number of them Nancy inquired without success about the missing dancer. It was not until she reached the village of Hopewell that fortune favoured her.

At her father's suggestion, she ran into the local police station. As the girl started to tell the desk sergeant her problem, a middle-aged woman in outmoded clothes bustled in. The newcomer was Mrs. Speyer, known as the town gossip. Ignoring Nancy, she pushed her way to the desk.

"Sergeant, you must do something right away!" she berated him in a rasping voice. "Such a shiftless police force as this town has!"

"What's wrong this time, Mrs. Speyer?" the man asked wearily.

"Three of my best laying hens have been stolen! That's what's wrong. I want the thief caught and punished."

"Are you sure the hens weren't taken by a weasel?"

"A weasel?" Mrs. Speyer tossed her head angrily. "The very idea!"

"Farmer Hopper at the edge of town lost a dozen chickens that way," the sergeant disclosed. "My advice to you is to go home and set a trap."

Nancy, who at first had been annoyed by the interruption, now was secretly amused. Mrs. Speyer flounced about, insisting that her hens had been taken by a thief. When her complaint had no effect upon the sergeant, she threatened to report him to the Chief of Police.

"Go right ahead," the officer encouraged her. "It's your privilege."

Decidedly nettled, Mrs. Speyer subsided into injured silence. She started to leave the police station, but changed her mind. Having observed Nancy at the desk, she was curious to learn what the stranger's buisness might be in town. Paying no attention to Mrs. Speyer, the girl told the sergeant why she had stopped at Hopewell.

"I wish I could help you," he replied regretfully. "I'll make a full report of the matter, and if we discover anything, I'll notify you."

"Is there no one in the force who might remember if Florianna Johnson ever came here?" Nancy asked.

"Afraid not, Miss. Even our Chief has held office only eight years."

Mrs. Speyer edged closer. "Sergeant," she said, "I can probably help this young lady. Don't you remember that beautiful, well-dressed woman who came here about ten years ago? The one that was hit by an automobile and taken to the hospital?"

"Never heard about it," the sergeant retorted gruffly, but he did get down from the desk and go off to look up some records.

"Funny thing," he said, coming back presently. "The young woman you mention is listed here, all right, but it says 'No Identification.' I guess if she had a bag, her name wasn't in it."

"No doubt she was unconscious when she was picked up," said Nancy. "But wouldn't the police have gotten her name later?"

"Not if she didn't make any claim against the fellow that hit her. And she couldn't do that," added the sergeant, " 'cause he was a hit-and-run driver."

"Maybe the hospital will know the woman's name," suggested Nancy.

"I knew the nurse who took care of her," Mrs. Speyer spoke up. "Her name was Emily Foster. She told me she suspected her patient didn't give her right name to the hospital authorities when she was leaving."

Here was real information which warranted investigation, Nancy decided! She asked where she could find Emily Foster.

"Oh, Emily went away years ago," was the discouraging reply. "I couldn't tell you where. She promised to write to me but she never did."

"Perhaps I can find out at the hospital," said Nancy.

Thanking Mrs. Speyer and the sergeant for their help, the Drew girl left the police station. Accompanied by her father, she called at the local hospital. The superintendent of the institution received them courteously and upon hearing their story, placed certain records at their disposal. No one by the name of either Flossie or Florianna Johnson had been a patient at the institution.

"She may have used an assumed name," Nancy sighed. "Her nurse inferred as much."

"Florianna was trying to get away from her public for a while," Mr. Drew added thoughtfully.

"You might talk to Joe," the superintendent suggested. "He's an old coloured man who's been with us for twenty years. A friendly fellow. And his memory for patients is amazing."

Joe was on the first floor of the hospital, scrubbing the corridor tiles. When Mr. Drew described Florianna to him, a wide grin spread over the old man's face.

"Indeed Ah does remembeh dat gal! Ah felt pow'ful sorry when she went out o' heah in dat wheel chaiah. She was cryin' her eyes out when I rolled 'er to de elevator."

"The woman left in a wheel chair?" Mr. Drew inquired quickly. "Was she crippled?"

"She was, boss. Ah ovah-headed Doc Barnes tell her she wouldn't neveh walk much again."

"Is Doctor Barnes still with the hospital?"

"No, boss. Doc went to a New York hospital where dey made him de big head man."

Joe's information threw an interesting new light on the mystery. Though Nancy and her father could not be certain that the crippled patient had been Florianna, they were inclined to think she had been. If such were the case, perhaps they had stumbled upon an explanation for her strange disappearance.

"Such an injury would have prevented Florianna from ever dancing again," Nancy said. "That knowledge would have crushed her pride. Wouldn't it have been natural for her to take an assumed name and drop out of sight?"

"Florianna would have done exactly that, I feel sure," Mr. Drew agreed. "She never would have wanted to burden her sister or her aunt with caring for her."

"And if she were a cripple, her foolish pride wouldn't have allowed her to marry Walter Heath," Nancy added. "Oh, Dad, I feel as if we really are getting somewhere on the case now!"

At the main desk, Nancy and her father tried without

success to obtain a better identification of the crippled woman.

"Emily Foster took care of her," Nancy volunteered. "She could tell us something, perhaps. Do you know her address?"

"The one I have is old, and I understand she left the place some time ago. However, the people who live there ought to be able to tell you where she is."

Nancy was grateful for the address. While her father registered at a hotel, she hopefully hurried to the designated house which stood at the edge of the town in a secluded spot. To her disappointment, she found the residence occupied by new tenants who never had heard of an Emily Foster!

"Another blind alley!" Nancy sighed as she started back to join her father. "I never knew clues to be more elusive."

As the girl walked along the street, she became aware of someone walking a little distance behind her. At first she thought nothing of it, but after she had covered three blocks, she concluded he must be following her.

"I don't like this!" Nancy thought, quickening her pace.

When she had walked six blocks more, and he was still behind her, the girl decided to obtain a good look at the fellow. She pretended to drop her purse. Turning quickly as if to pick it up, she gazed directly at the man. He wore a brown suit and had a sharp, angular face marked with a mole. Realizing that Nancy knew she was being followed, he wheeled and turned down a side street.

"He *was* trailing me!" the girl thought. "I wonder why."

Nancy had never seen the man before, and she kept worrying about the matter. She intended to speak to her father about it, but found that he had invited a friend to dinner. By ten o'clock, after a jolly evening, she had forgotten the incident.

Before retiring, father and daughter both sat down in Mr. Drew's bedroom to discuss the mystery. Nancy at once brought up the subject of Emily Foster.

"Don't you agree she's our best lead yet?" the girl asked.

Mr. Drew did not answer; in fact, for several seconds he had not been paying strict attention to what his daughter had been saying. Now, so suddenly that Nancy was startled, he tiptoed to the hall door of the room. As she watched in bewilderment, he gave the knob a quick, deft twist.

The door swung inward. A man in a brown suit was crouching just outside! Thrown off balance, he fell forward into the room.

Chapter XV

BEHIND THE DOOR

"So you were eavesdropping!" Mr. Drew sternly accused the man who had been listening at the door, as he pulled him roughly to his feet.

"No, that's not true," the fellow stammered. Recovering his balance, he tried to retreat. Mr. Drew blocked the doorway.

"Sit down," he ordered. "We want to talk to you."

Nancy was glad her father intended to question the man. She recognized him as the one who had followed her.

"What were you doing at the door?" Mr. Drew asked him sharply.

"Nothing," he replied in a sullen voice. "I thought this room belonged to a friend of mine."

"I'm afraid that's rather hard to believe, for you had your ear to the keyhole when I opened the door. Tell me your name."

"It's none of your business."

"I can turn you over to the police."

"And I can report to them that you trailed me today," said Nancy.

The stranger looked worried and squirmed uneasily in the chair. "You can't prove it!"

"This man followed you today?" Mr. Drew questioned his daughter in surprise.

"Yes, I forgot to tell you about it."

"Then that settles it!" the lawyer announced grimly. "We'll turn this fellow over to the police for questioning."

"No, no, don't do that! I'll tell you anything you want to know—except my name!" The eavesdropper could not know that Mr. Drew's threat to call the police was only a bluff.

"Very well," nodded the lawyer. "Why were you following my daughter this afternoon?"

"I followed her because I was to be paid a good wad to do it."

"By whom?"

"I'm not saying. Anyhow, I don't know the guy's name."

"What were your instructions?"

The fellow hung his head and refused to reply until the lawyer referred again to the police. "I was told to make a complete report on where she went, who she talked to, and what she did."

Mr. Drew turned so that the man could not see him. With a quick movement of his hand and a jerk of his eyebrows, he signalled for Nancy to step into her bedroom. For a moment the girl was puzzled. Then it dawned upon her that her father probably wanted her to slip quietly downstairs and make arrangements to have the stranger trailed.

"So you won't tell us your name?" Mr. Drew repeated, gazing significantly at Nancy.

"No, I won't," the man retorted.

Nancy stole noiselessly from the room. Hastening downstairs, she used one of the public telephones to call the police station. Identifying her father and herself, she said:

"Please send a plainclothes detective at once. I'll meet him in the lobby here and explain everything to him when he arrives. How will I know him?"

"He'll pretend to be lame."

Nancy was worried lest the detective might not reach the

hotel in time. In less than five minutes, however, a limping man walked in. The Drew girl told him why he had been called. She asked that he trail the eavesdropper when he should leave the hotel.

"Here he comes now!" she whispered, as the brown-suited stranger emerged from an elevator. "I'll get out of sight! He mustn't see me!"

Nancy secreted herself behind a pillar. She was pleased to observe that when the detective followed the culprit from the hotel, the latter appeared to be unaware of it.

"I hope that's what Dad expected me to do," Nancy thought, stepping into the elevator.

Mr. Drew was waiting at the door to his room. He assured his daughter that she had interpreted his signals correctly. The stranger, he reported, had been too nervous to notice the girl's absence.

"By the way," Mr. Drew asked, as they sat down, "have you telephoned to Mrs. Gruen since we left home, Nancy? There may be messages for us."

The girl admitted that she had forgotten to do so.

"You'd better put in a long-distance call right away," her father urged.

The call was placed, and after a brief interval Nancy heard Hannah's familiar voice.

"How glad I am you phoned," she said at once. "I tried to reach you at Hampton, but the hotel clerk said you had left."

"Is anything wrong?"

"Mrs. Fenimore was here this morning. She wanted to see you very much."

"Mrs. Fenimore?" Nancy echoed in surprise. Knowing that the invalid seldom left her cottage, she realized that only an urgent matter would have prompted the woman to undertake the trip.

"She wouldn't explain why she came," Mrs. Gruen resumed. "When I told her you weren't at home, she said you must be warned to be careful."

"Careful of what?"

"She seemed to think you're in danger. Oh, Nancy, I'll be so relieved when you're home again safe and sound."

"We'll be back tomorrow," the girl reassured the housekeeper. "Don't worry about me."

Nancy speculated as to why Mrs. Fenimore considered her to be in danger. Could the woman have learned that she was to be shadowed by the mysterious man in brown?

Nancy and Mr. Drew waited until midnight for a report from the plainclothesman. When he failed to return to the hotel, they telephoned police headquarters. The detective had not checked in yet. In the morning there still was no word, so Mr. Drew requested that a full report of the matter be forwarded to him at River Heights.

Nancy lost no time in calling at the Fenimore cottage after she arrived home the next afternoon. The woman was reclining on a couch, exhausted from the strain and worry of the previous day.

"I shouldn't have allowed myself to become so upset," she said to Nancy after she had greeted the girl. "But Hector Keep always affects me that way."

"Then he came here to see you?"

"I had a dreadful session with him. He asked me so many questions."

"About your sister?"

"Yes, he wanted to know if I had engaged anyone to search for Florianna."

"Did you mention my name?"

"Well, I did say you had offered to help me," Mrs. Fenimore admitted, "though I felt unhappy about having told him. From the way Mr. Keep acted, I'm sure he intends to make trouble for you."

"I'm not afraid of Hector Keep," Nancy said defiantly.

"Oh, but you should have heard him talk! He said he wouldn't let anyone meddle in his affairs. He seems to think Heath Castle belongs to him!"

"Mr. Keep is worried," Nancy commented, frowning. "His remarks make it perfectly clear to me that he has a guilty conscience."

"Will you risk going to Heath Castle again?"

"I'll certainly return there if it will accomplish anything," Nancy said with determination. "But I believe the mystery may be solved in another way."

She thought it best not to tell Mrs. Fenimore about the possibility that her sister might have been crippled as the result of an automobile accident. She merely said there was an interesting new lead to follow, one which would not involve her coming in contact with the troublesome Mr. Keep.

Immediately upon returning home, Nancy took stock of the mystery. Thieves probably were prowling around the Heath grounds, looking for something important. Did it have anything to do with Florianna? Was Hector Keep up to some underhand work in connection with it?

"And then there's Emily Foster, and the man who was eavesdropping——"

As Nancy opened the top drawer of her bureau to get a handkerchief, she spied the torn half-note she had found in the debris at the Heath factory. In the recent excitement she had forgotten all about it.

"This may turn out to be my most valuable clue," she berated herself. "I must try to figure it out."

She sat down at once to piece out the message, but had hardly started when the telephone rang. The caller was George, wanting to know how the solution to the mystery was progressing.

"I have a clue to your stolen clothes," the Drew girl laughed, and told of having seen a shirt similar to George's on Mrs. Hooker's clothesline.

"Why, the nerve of that woman!" her chum exclaimed indignantly. "I'm going there at once and demand that she give up my property!"

"You can't prove anything, George," Nancy discouraged her. "Better forget the matter for the time being, and come over here. I have lots to tell you. Bring Bess along."

"Be there pronto," George replied.

As Nancy returned to her room, she said to herself, "If it

was Jeddy who took those clothes, what was *he* doing in the Heath gardens? Is it possible that boy is connected with the mystery?"

She was still trying to figure this out when the other girls arrived. Nancy told them everything that had happened on the trip with her father.

"Poor Florianna!" Bess exclaimed. "How dreadful for a wonderful dancer to have her career cut off that way!"

"I wish you could have found that nurse Emily Foster," George added. "But maybe she isn't even alive today. Well, what are you going to work on next, Nancy?"

"This note, or rather, this piece of a note."

She produced the bit of paper, and together the girls pored over it for some time, each with a pencil and paper, trying to fill out the lines to form a logical message. Bess was the first one to claim having pieced together the missing words.

"Listen to this!" she cried gleefully. "I have it!"

"Let's hear it," urged Nancy.

> "Dear C,
>   Some place is the se-
> cret which I hid
> in a wall. I want to be
> famous. If I find it, it will be a
> worthy work."

George scoffed. "Nobody would write a note with such uneven lines. And we know already something is hidden in a wall."

"Well, it fills in the missing words," Bess defended herself.

"One guess is as good as another," Nancy said kindly.

For some little time the three girls continued their deciphering; at least, Bess and George did. Nancy meanwhile fell to dreaming. Suddenly she jumped up from her chair, saying:

"The solution to this mystery might lie in this very house!"

D

Without explaining her strange remark, she ran from the room and down the stairs. In a few minutes she returned, carrying a large book.

"How in the world are you going to find Florianna with that?" asked George.

What Nancy held was a portfolio of coloured pictures and descriptions of famous old houses and gardens in England. Knowing of the girl's interest in gardening, a cousin of Nancy's had sent the book to her several Christmases before.

"I forgot I had these pictures," she said, quickly turning the leaves. "Girls, look here!"

"Heath Castle!" exclaimed George.

"The original one in England. Only of course it wasn't called Heath!"

"And the gardens!" cried Bess, as they looked at picture after picture.

Nancy was busy reading the description of them, when suddenly a paragraph caught her eye.

"Oh, George! Bess! Listen to this! At last I think we have the clue we've been looking for!"

Chapter XVI

THE SEARCH RESUMED

GEORGE and Bess studied the paragraph to which Nancy had pointed. It was a quotation in Old English, and they could not make it out. Nancy, who had learned to read the works of the old English poet Chaucer in school, eagerly translated it.

" 'I have hid my treasures in the niches of the cloister through which, all unsuspecting, the gay man and fair ladies pass each day to bathe,' " she read.

"Sounds quaint," said Bess, "but how does it help us? Those words were written a long time ago about people who visited at the English castle, I suppose, and walked through a cloister in the garden to go bathing."

"Why, don't you see!" Nancy cried excitedly. "Ira Heath built his estate here to resemble the one in England. Probably both he and his son knew about the cloister."

"Granted," nodded George. "But where's our clue, Nancy?"

"If the Heaths had a treasure to hide, wouldn't *their* cloister have been a good place in which to put it?"

" 'I have hid my treasures in the niches of the cloister,' " George repeated the words softly. "Is there a cloister in the Heath gardens? I haven't seen one."

Nancy turned the page and the three girls gazed thoughtfully at the picture on it, which showed a long passageway flanked by columns leading toward a river.

"This is it," said Nancy. "Oh, I wonder if there is one at Heath Castle!"

"You didn't notice it from the air or when you were in the tower?" Bess inquired.

"N-no," answered Nancy slowly. "But there was something leading from the castle toward the river—a kind of tunnel covered with vines."

"I'll bet that's it," said George enthusiastically. "Listen!" she commanded suddenly. "Here comes somebody who might be able to tell us!"

From down the street came the strains of a familiar song. Presently the singer turned into the Drew driveway. He warbled,

> "Clams by the bushel,
> Clams by the lot,
> Clams for the kettle,
> Clams for the pot."

"Nancy," George continued, "I'll bet Mehearty can tell you about a cloister at the Heath estate if it runs down to the water. That old sailor knows every inch of the Muskoka River."

"It won't hurt to ask him," agreed Nancy.

By the time the girls reached the kitchen door, Hannah Gruen was about to step outside to look in Mehearty's basket.

"Why I keep buying that man's clams I don't know," she muttered. "No telling where he gets them—certainly not from a protected bed. I wouldn't risk eating one of them raw."

Despite her remark, the housekeeper purchased twice as many clams for chowder as she needed, and carried them into the house. Looking up, the jolly old fisherman noticed Nancy in the doorway.

"And how are ye, me lass?" he asked, smiling. "Sorry I can't give ye any report about that fellow what crashed into ye. I been lookin' high and low for his boat, but I ain't seen any part of her, fore nor aft."

The clam digger asked the girl, a twinkle in his eyes, if she would like to take another trip to the Heath factory.

"No, thank you," Nancy laughed. "No more explosions for me! But, Mehearty, I *am* thinking of going to the Heath gardens by boat. Have you ever noticed a—a sort of tunnel there, leading from the beach?"

"Never have noticed any," the clam digger replied. "How do ye figure on gettin' to the place by boat? A motorboat couldn't get near the beach nowadays, and it's too far for ye to row all the way from here."

Nancy's mind worked fast. "Perhaps some time when you're not busy, Mehearty——" she began.

The old sailor suddenly slapped his thigh and chuckled. "By the Great Horned Spoon, I allus said women'd never come right out and ask for things. Miss Nancy, me lass," he added, "I'll meet ye and those friends o' yours at th' Landin' ten o'clock sharp tomorrow mornin', barrin' rain. You rent a motorboat, an' we'll tie my little dinghy to it. When we get to th' Heath place, I'll row ye ashore an' ye can hunt for that tunnel."

Nancy smiled her pleasure at the plan, and thanked the kindly old sailor. Turning to Bess and George, she learned they could go with her, so arrangements were made for the trip.

As Mehearty started away, Nancy suddenly stopped him, saying she had something to show him. From the pockets of her riding breeches, the girl retrieved a few whelk shells she had scooped out of the pond in the Heath gardens.

"Is this the kind that contains the valuable dye?" Nancy asked the man.

"Sure is," the old fellow said enthusiastically. "Where'd ye get 'em?"

Nancy told him. When the clam digger heard about the number to be found in the pond, he whistled.

"Now that's mighty interestin'," he declared, deeply impressed. "In the old days fortunes were made in whelk dye. Maybe the Heaths made part o' theirs that way. Who knows?"

"I rather doubt that," Nancy said, "but I'm curious to find out about Walt's experiments along that line."

"Ye can, if ye've a mind to."

"How?"

"Old Sam Weatherby can tell ye what ye want to know."

"The curio dealer?"

"Sam worked at the Heath factory afore he went into business for himself. He knew Walt as well as anyone in town."

"Then Sam Weatherby is the man I'll see," Nancy said gleefully, grateful for the information.

Soon after Mehearty had gone down the street, Bess and George left for home, telling Nancy they would be on hand the next morning. The Drew girl decided to make good use of the intervening time by calling upon Sam Weatherby. The old curio dealer was polishing a pewter teapot as the young detective entered his cluttered little shop.

"Haven't seen you for several days," he greeted her cheerfully. "Did you bring that pearl and the shell I offered to buy?"

Nancy ruefully told him she no longer had them, and why.

"That's too bad," the old man sympathized upon hearing the pearl had been stolen. "Well, maybe you'll find a bigger one."

"I hope so," Nancy smiled, "but right now I'm more interested in dye than in pearls. Do you know whether Walter Heath ever did any experimental work with whelk dye?"

The question surprised the old curio dealer, because he considered himself one of the few people who knew this fact.

"Walt Heath had an idea he could use whelk dye in the manufacture of coloured pearl buttons," he disclosed. "In that way he hoped to give his waning business a spurt."

"His experiments were carried on at the factory?"

"No, at Heath Castle. He never perfected them enough to use the process at the factory. But his experimental work brought him luck, just the same."

"How was that, Mr. Weatherby?"

"Well, he found a big pearl; at least, that's what he told me. Said he was going to present it to a young lady friend of his—a dancer."

Nancy blinked in astonishment at the revelation. Perhaps young Mr. Heath had not had time to give it to Florianna before she disappeared. Maybe he had hidden it in one of the walls. Possibly in a niche in the cloister wall!

"At least I'm sure of one thing," she reflected. "Walter Heath experimented in dye making. He may have perfected a very fine variety, and hid bottles of it away to keep them secret until he was ready to use them."

Nancy was convinced now that she knew the reason why mysterious strangers prowled about the old factory and the estate grounds. They were searching either for the pearl or for the bottles of dye, possibly both. One of the men she had overheard while in the tower had spoken of being satisfied with what they already had found.

Thanking the curio dealer for his information, Nancy turned to leave. An object in the show case caught her eye.

Resting in a velvet case was the antique watch charm she knew Mr. Weatherby had bought from Hector Keep.

"Handsome, isn't it?" the old man inquired, removing the charm from its case. "An old English family design. A genuine heirloom."

Nancy admired the piece of jewellery. Mr. Weatherby also showed her a pair of earrings, a bracelet and a brooch, all bearing the same design.

"Hector Keep sold me the entire set," the dealer revealed. "That lawyer is a hard customer, though. He haggles for the last penny."

"You say Mr. Keep inherited these from English ancestors?" Nancy asked.

"That's what he said. Between you and me, I think he picked them up from a client who couldn't pay a bill."

Nancy did not disclose her own thought on the subject. Had Hector Keep come honestly by the watch charm and the other pieces of jewellery? The girl told herself sternly that she must not mistrust the lawyer because she disliked him.

When Nancy reached home, she learned that during her absence a long-distance telephone call had come from Hopewell. Either she or her father was to get in touch with the man who had telephoned.

"He was a detective," Mrs. Gruen told her, "and he wouldn't give me the message."

Nancy put in the call to the police station at Hopewell and identified herself. The plainclothes man was out at the time, but had left his report for her. The stranger he had shadowed the night before had driven to River Heights. From there he had gone on to meet another man at the abandoned Heath button factory.

"If I only knew who that person is!" Nancy exclaimed.

"I have a description of him," said the police sergeant, reading it.

From the description of the strange man, the girl was almost certain he was the same fellow she suspected had damaged the motorboat she had rented.

"Our detective said to tell you he was sorry he had to come back to Hopewell without learning more," the policeman concluded, "but of course it's really out of his territory. We suggest that you have the River Heights police help you from now on."

Nancy thanked the man, saying her father would get in touch with him later. For several hours, in fact until bedtime, she kept trying to figure out this latest angle to the puzzle. Her father was to be away overnight, so she could not discuss the matter with him. She did talk it over with Hannah Gruen, but that good woman had nothing to offer except advice about the girl using caution in her sleuthing.

Nancy was up early the next morning. She was the first of those who planned the trip to Heath Castle to arrive at the Landing. By telephone she had made arrangements to rent the same motorboat she had had before. The owner assured her it had been repaired and was in first-class shape.

George came next, then Bess. Finally Mehearty showed up in his rowboat, which he fastened securely to the larger one.

"All set," he announced. "Cast off!"

Nancy asked the old man if he wanted to do the piloting, but he sheepishly admitted that he'd never learned how. "Me for sailin' ships and such," he said.

The girls enjoyed the ride upstream; not only because it was beautiful on the river, but because the old clam digger was very entertaining with his sea songs and exaggerated stories. He told one story about a sailor's ghost so realistically that it made the chills go down Bess's spine.

"Coming to Heath Castle," the old man announced suddenly, pointing to a wild-looking spot ahead.

In the distance the girls could see the high turrets, and Nancy recalled the man she had seen signalling from one of them with a flashlight. His helper probably had been on the water. Presently Mehearty told her to turn off the motor; they would row the rest of the way.

The shore line was matted thickly with bushes, and only a

narrow beach was visible. Above it stood a high, weather-stained wall—the river barrier of Heath Castle.

"How can we ever get in?" Bess gasped, observing the height of the wall.

"You haven't forgotten about a possible opening, have you?" asked Nancy.

The old clam digger assisted the girls into the rowboat and untied it from the anchored motorboat. With powerful strokes, he sent the little craft surging through the water. Presently it grounded on the shore, and they all stepped out.

"My, my," said Mehearty. "Judgin' from them little blow holes in the sand, I'd say there are clams aplenty here."

The old man began digging. The eager girls started toward the wall. Not one of the group gave a thought to the fact that an unfriendly person might be coming there and would discover them. But about two miles down the stream, and heading for Heath Castle, was a figure in a boat, rocking back and forth over his oars as he rowed closer and closer to Nancy and her friends.

Chapter XVII

A POCKET IN THE WALL

LEAVING the old sailor to explore the beach, the three girls turned their attention to the high retaining wall which marked the rear boundary of the Heath estate. Only the treetops in the gardens above them were visible. Directly in front of the stone wall grew tall brier bushes.

"We'll never be able to get over," Bess Marvin declared, as she followed her chums along the sand, "and I don't see any steps. Hello, what's this?" she cried all of a sudden.

The girl had spied something half buried in the sand. Examination revealed that it was George's lost riding breeches. When their owner saw the condition they were in, she announced she never would wear them again.

Nancy was thoughtful. "That boy who took them. He just seemed to appear on the beach out of nowhere."

She paused. Bess and George waited expectantly.

"I don't recall seeing the boy scale a wall," Nancy continued after a moment. "He must have reached the beach in some other way."

"You mean by the cloister?" asked Bess, staring at the crumbling wall.

"Maybe. I'm sure there's an opening of some kind along here."

Pushing ahead, Nancy began to examine the base of the wall. In many places bushes and young trees had grown out from it, anchoring their roots in the cracks between the stones.

Marsh flies made life miserable for the girls, and briers scratched them unmercifully. Bess was all for giving up the search. Even Nancy became discouraged, though she would not admit it.

"That boy came through here," she insisted stubbornly. "There must be a passageway, and we're going to find it!"

Her determination was rewarded. Twenty yards farther on she parted some brier bushes, and saw revealed several large stones which apparently never had been cemented into the wall. She pushed against the centre one. To her surprise, it moved easily.

"Girls, this may be the entranceway!" she cried.

Nancy pressed against the stone. It fell inward, to reveal a flight of eight steps leading upward to an arched passageway.

"The cloister!" Nancy cried gleefully.

To enlarge the entrance hole, she pushed against another stone. At first it would not move. Then suddenly it gave way, weakening a whole section of the wall. A great mass of debris came tumbling down upon the girls.

Nancy seized George's arm, jerking her backwards barely in time to miss being struck by the stones. Bess, scrambling to escape, lost her balance and fell into a thorn bush, scratching herself painfully.

"Oh, girls, I'm terribly sorry!" Nancy apologized. "It was all my fault for moving the stone."

"I hope the entrance isn't blocked," said George.

There still was an opening, though barely large enough for a person to squeeze through. Nancy scrambled inside and led the way up the flight of stone steps. At the top, the trio paused to catch their breaths.

"How beautiful!" exclaimed Bess. "It was worth all the trouble! Why, this is like a place one dreams about."

Before them stretched a long, flagstone passageway. One side of it was set with square columns built of stone. Between these grew the heavy stalks of vines which formed a solid roof of leaves. The other side of the cloister was a solid stone wall with deep insets at intervals of twenty-five feet.

"Just like the picture we saw in the book!" Nancy cried in delight. "Oh, what an attractive walk to a bathing beach!"

"Now to find the hidden treasure!" cried George. "Come on!"

Hopefully the girls examined the insets along the wall, some of which had built-in stone shelves. In one, a statuette lay on its side; in another, a broken vase had tipped over.

"Nothing here——" Bess started to say as she reached the next one, only to break off.

Nancy had held up a finger in warning. "Listen!" she whispered.

At the girl's command, both Bess and George stood still. Faintly, they could hear men's voices. The sounds came from the other side of the wall, some little distance away.

Cautiously the girls stole along the flagstones, hardly daring to breathe. As they reached another niche, the deep voices came to them distinctly.

"This looks like a good spot!" a man said, making no attempt to speak low. "Let's have your pick, Cobb."

With a start, Nancy realized that the man on the other side of the wall intended to do more destruction there. The voices were strangely familiar. Where had she heard them before? Suddenly she knew.

She had heard them the night of her imprisonment in the tower!

The men fell to work with chisel, pick, and sledge hammer. Tiny stones and bits of mortar rattled down at the girls' feet.

"They're wrecking this lovely wall!" George whispered indignantly to her chums. "Oh, I'm tempted to tell them to stop!"

"We're trespassers here," Bess reminded her. "They may have been ordered to do the work. Don't say anything."

As the three friends waited, a decorative ledge loosened itself from the wall niche. Repeated blows from the other side of the barrier threatened to send it crashing to the flagstone floor. Unable to witness such wanton destruction, Nancy stepped forward to catch the ledge as it fell. With Bess's help, she laid it carefully on the ground.

Straightening up, the Drew girl gazed at the wall niche, now disfigured. What she saw caused her to draw in her breath sharply. Where the ledge had been, there now was revealed a long, narrow pocket!

Scarcely daring to hope, Nancy ran her hand into the dark opening. Her groping fingers touched something hard.

A box!

"Nancy!" George warned tensely.

Directly above the girl's hand a stone chisel was poking through the wall. The men on the other side of the wall were working diligently. In another moment they would succeed in making a large opening into the niche.

Nancy did not wait to be discovered. She seized the heavy box, and with the other girls turned and fled along the cloister. For a time they could hear the two men working on the wall; then gradually the sounds died away.

"We're safe," Nancy exclaimed. "Now let's open the box!"

Chapter XVIII

POET'S NOOK

So excited that her hands trembled, Nancy lifted the lid of the rusty metal box. Were the Heath pearl and other jewels inside? But the girls were to be disappointed at the contents, for the box appeared to contain only papers and photographs.

"Oh, why would anyone bother to hide such things!" Bess exclaimed, completely let down. "There's nothing valuable here. And after all our trouble, too."

"We mustn't be too hasty," cautioned Nancy. "We haven't looked through the things yet."

Carefully she lifted out the top photograph. The picture was an old one, yellowed with age, and contained traces of mould. It showed a half pose of a middle-aged man with side whiskers. At the bottom was scrawled the name "Ira Heath," and a date.

Nancy was about to hand the picture to George, when a detail of the old estate owner's clothing caught her attention. A watch chain which hung from Mr. Heath's vest pocket had an unusual charm attached to it.

"Girls, notice that watch charm!" she cried. "I saw the very same thing at Sam Weatherby's curio shop!"

"How did it get there?" Bess asked, studying the photograph. "Do you suppose he sold it to Mr. Weatherby before his death?"

"Nothing of the sort. Hector Keep sold it to him along with some other jewellery."

"Hector Keep!" George exclaimed in surprise. "Then you think——"

"I don't know what to think, George," Nancy admitted. "There's always the possibility that the charm was given to Mr. Keep. But in that case, there wouldn't have been any reason for his pretending it was an heirloom of his own family. That's what he told Mr. Weatherby."

"It certainly sounds suspicious," George said, reaching for another photograph. "Oh, here's an old-fashioned one!"

She held up the picture of a sweet-faced woman in a long velvet gown with a bustle. An inscription identified her as Ira Heath's wife Ida. The woman's dark hair was worn high, exposing shapely ears which were set off with earrings of unique design.

"Those earrings!" Nancy exclaimed when she saw them. "They're at Mr. Weatherby's shop too! Oh, now I *am* suspicious!"

There were other pictures in the box, but the girls passed over them quickly as they were of no particular interest. An article that did hold their attention was a small, leather-bound diary. The fly-leaf bore Walter Heath's name, and the dates of many of the notations showed they had been made not many months before his death.

"This may be what's really valuable in this box!" Nancy declared jubilantly.

Rapidly she skimmed through the small book. Many of the pages were blank, but under one date she came to an item important enough to read aloud.

"'Stumbled upon something which may prove to be a treasure. Whelks are right on the shores of Heath Castle. They contain a beautiful magenta dye. Am mixing it with various chemicals. So far I've produced six shades of fast-colour dye.'"

"This proves that your theory about Walter Heath's experiments was right, Nancy," George said in praise.

"I wonder what became of the dye?" the Drew girl mused, thumbing through the little book. "Mehearty said that in the old days magenta dye brought high prices. Dyed wool sold for more than two hundred dollars a pound."

"Read on," urged Bess impatiently. "Maybe we'll learn what became of the dye."

Unmindful of the men whom the girls had heard on the

other side of the cloister, Nancy searched for another important notation.

"Here's something!" she cried a moment later. "Listen to this:

" 'I don't trust the new chauffeur Biggs. Have decided to hide all the bottles of magenta dye until my experiments are complete.' "

"Does it say where he hid them?" George demanded. "Read the next page."

"There doesn't seem to be anything more. That was the last paragraph in the book."

"Oh, what a shame!" Bess wailed.

"I skimmed over the first part. Maybe I'll find other clues when I read the entire diary carefully. But there's no time now."

"I'll say there isn't!" agreed George. "Sh! We'd better duck out of here—and fast!"

From just across the stone barrier came the barking of a dog. Voices were audible, and each moment they grew louder. The two workmen were approaching!

"How about looking on the opposite side of this wall?" they heard one of the men ask his companion.

"O.K., agreed the other. "May as well make a good job of it while we're here."

Fearful lest they be seen, the girls sped on tiptoe along the cloistered walk, Nancy carrying the metal box.

"We should have gone the other way, toward the beach," she whispered belatedly. "We may trap ourselves this way!"

Her prediction proved to be only too correct. A hundred yards farther on, the cloister abruptly ended at one of the castle walls. The door leading into the big dwelling was locked.

"Oh, what'll we do?" Bess asked uneasily. "This is awful."

The men had climbed the wall and now were moving slowly up the flagstone passageway. In a moment or two they certainly would see the girls.

"Nancy, we'll have to hide the box!" George said, listening to the approaching footsteps.

"A better idea would be to hide ourselves," Bess whispered. "But where?"

Not far from the castle wall was a nook of considerable size. In their haste, the girls had passed it with little more than a fleeting glance. Now, in looking about for a place of concealment, Nancy saw that it offered possibilities.

"Follow me!" she directed her companions.

Above the arched entrance to the refuge had been chiselled the words "Poet's nook," but the girls scarcely noticed this, as they slipped into the hiding place barely an instant before the two workmen came into view.

"I must hide this box so those men can't take it, even if they catch us!" Nancy whispered grimly.

Frantically the girls looked about them for a place to hide the precious metal box. There seemed to be none. Then Nancy noticed a loose stone in the wall directly above a bench at the back of the niche. Almost without hope, she asked George to see if it would move.

The stone came out, revealing an empty space behind it. Fortunately the recess was large enough to hold the metal box. Nancy slipped it inside, and George quickly fitted the stone back into place.

By this time the men were very near, and had stopped walking. Nancy wanted to peer from the nook, but recognized the folly of trying to see the men. With her chums she flattened herself against the wall beyond the opening and waited.

"How about working in that Poet's Nook?" one of the men asked suddenly. "Maybe we'll find something there."

Nancy, Bess, and George waited with bated breaths for the answer.

"We looked there once. That hiding place over the bench was empty."

"Sure, but if we take out the whole wall, we might find another hiding place. You're lazy if you ask me, Cobb."

"Did I ask you?" the other growled. "Swinging a pick is hard work. We're not getting any too much money for it, either."

The other laughed. "What we found already is good enough pay for me. And if we find the other thing, we can live on Easy Street."

Nancy and her chums relaxed slightly, thinking that the men would not search the Poet's Nook a second time. But their hopes were dashed.

"How about it?" the first man demanded. "Do we take out the wall or don't we?"

"O.K.," the one addressed as Cobb replied. "You go ahead. I'll be with you in a minute."

Chapter XIX

CINDERELLA'S SLIPPER

PICKING up a sledge hammer, Cobb's partner started toward the Poet's Nook. Nancy, Bess, and George sought to melt into the shadows, but they knew they could not escape detection!

"Be with you in a minute, Biggs," Cobb called. "I want to see if there's anything hidden in this niche."

Biggs! The name elecrified the three girls. Hadn't Walter Heath named him in the diary as a suspicious person? Could he be the chauffeur, searching, perhaps, for the bottles of dye his former employer had secreted on the premises?

Biggs now was just outside the Poet's Nook. Nancy and her friends gave up all hope of escaping detection. Then, just as the fellow was about to enter, running footsteps could be heard along the flagstones. Startled, the man paused and looked down the cloister.

Nancy tiptoed forward and peeked out. Biggs was the one who had signalled from the tower! She was just in time to see a boy who was gesticulating wildly toward the beach.

"Hey! Come quick!" the lad shouted. "I've got something to show you!"

Cobb was irritated. "Drat that boy!" he muttered. "How did he get here? We told him to keep away from Heath Castle." As the youngster came closer, gasping for breath, the man began to berate him. "You know better than to come here again! I told you not to follow me."

"I've got something to tell you!"

"Out with it!"

"Not on your life," the boy retorted craftily. "You got to pay me."

"Get out of here and leave us alone."

"Maybe we'd better hear what he has to say," Biggs urged. "It may be important."

"Gimme a quarter and I'll tell you," the boy demanded. "Not a cent less."

Biggs and Cobb were worried. The latter took a coin from his pocket and tossed it angrily at the boy.

"There!" he snapped. "Now what have you got to tell us?"

"Part of the beach wall has been knocked down. Someone came through the hole in it too."

"How do you know that?" Biggs demanded tensely.

"Footprints on the ground. Want to see 'em?"

"Guess we'd better," Cobb nodded, a feeling of concern taking the place of his anger. "If anyone's on these premises, we'd better find out about it!"

"If the place is being watched, I'm clearing out of here!" Biggs added in fright.

"Don't be a sap!" Cobb retorted. "If anyone came into the gardens through this passage, he's got to go out the same way. All we have to do is guard the hole in the wall and we'll catch him."

"I'm not so sure," muttered Biggs, "and I don't want to sit there all day and wait."

"What of it, if we catch the fellow?" demanded Cobb.

The two men followed the lad and soon were out of sight. When their voices died away, Nancy stepped cautiously from her hiding place.

"I believe that boy was Jeddy Hooker!" she declared excitedly. "I didn't see him very well, but from the glimpse I caught of him he certainly resembled Joan's playmate."

Bess was not so interested in this as in her own troubles. "Did you hear what those men said about guarding the exit?" she fretted. "How are we going to get out of here?"

"So long as the men stay on the beach, we're fairly safe," replied Nancy. "But I'm worried about Mehearty."

"That's so," agreed George, who had dropped down on the stone bench in the nook. "I forgot all about him. Oh, I hope they don't harm the poor man!"

As there was no way in which the girls could warn the clam digger, they considered their own plight. It seemed pretty serious.

"We can't go back to the beach," wailed Bess, "and we can't go on because the castle door is locked."

"There's one thing we can do," announced George suddenly, rising from the bench and stalking across the cloister.

"What's that?" asked Bess hopefully.

Her cousin pointed. Between two of the columns, intertwined with vines, were steps leading down into a small, tangled garden.

"See if there is a way out through here," George replied.

She and the others investigated the little garden, which had walls on each side, too high to scale. There was not a single opening in them. The girls had been defeated again!

"We're certainly in a tight spot," said George, wondering what their next move ought to be.

Bess sat down in the middle of a weed-grown path. "I'm so discouraged I could cry," she owned up.

"Maybe a drink of water will revive you," suggested her cousin practically.

On the rear wall of the garden was an artistic fountain from which spouted a little stream. Bess walked over to it and drank freely. "It's wonderful water," she announced, "and cool. It must be from a spring."

Nancy and George cupped their hands and filled them

several times. They agreed the water was unusually refreshing.

"Certainly gives you a lift," admitted Bess. "I feel now as if I wouldn't mind facing those men!"

Nancy suddenly noticed something on the crumbling wall just beneath the fountain. Parting some vines to get a better view, she stared in astonishment.

"Girls, look!" she cried. "On the wall!"

The vines had grown over a small block of cement which had been set into the stones. Visible on it was the imprint of a woman's slipper. Directly beneath appeared a single word:

Cinderella

"Cinderella's dancing slipper," George laughed. "Whoever would do such a crazy thing?"

"I'm not sure it was crazy," Nancy replied, her mind busily fitting together two pieces of the Heath puzzle. "I'd say it's romantic. It may have been Walter Heath's way of paying a compliment to someone."

"A story-book character?" asked Bess.

"No, a beautiful dancer named Florianna. Don't you recall that note I found in his handwriting which began 'Dear C'?"

"'C' could stand for Cinderella," George acknowledged. "It also could indicate a dozen other names."

Nancy measured the dainty little shoeprint with her hand. "Oh, I'm sure this is Florianna's!" she went on triumphantly. "It's the clue we need! And we found it in a crumbling old wall!"

Bess and George did not follow their friend's reasoning, and said so.

"I mean the clue Walter Heath mentioned in his will," Nancy explained. "He said Florianna would be able to identify herself in a special way! She could do it by means of this slipper print, couldn't she?"

"The shoe *is* very small," Bess admitted. "Not many girls could wear such a tiny size."

"Wouldn't anyone except Florianna know about this imprint in the wall?" asked George sceptically.

"Possibly," said Nancy. "But Florianna would be the only person to have proof she was the one he called Cinderella."

"You mean no impostor would have the shoe or other identification?" inquired George.

"Exactly."

"If you've really stumbled on a secret, Nancy, we mustn't breathe a word of it," said Bess, deeply impressed.

The three girls agreed to maintain absolute silence regarding the discovery. Carefully they covered the imprint with the vines, speculating as to whether anything of value might be hidden behind the cement block.

"We can't find out today," Nancy said. "We'd have to use tools to move it."

"It would be just our luck if Cobb and Biggs decide to smash the fountain!" George remarked. "Then we'd be too late." Suddenly she stiffened. "Listen!" she cried. "What's that?"

At the end of the cloister the castle door was opening with a groaning sound. Someone was coming out! Whoever it was would see them in another moment!

"Quick!" Nancy directed in a whisper. "Lie down here in the tall grass and weeds. It's our only chance!"

Bess and George flattened themselves on the ground. Nancy was able to dart behind a bush leafy enough for protection but not too thick for her to see through.

A man, slightly stooped, came walking with catlike tread along the flagstone cloister. He paused to examine the vines which Bess had disturbed near the steps. Nancy's heart stood still.

The man was Hector Keep!

The lawyer glanced toward the garden, but evidently saw no one, for he strode on toward the beach, his hands clasped behind him.

"Let's go!" Nancy whispered jubilantly a moment later. "The castle door may be open!" As the girls made a dash for it she added, "I'll get the metal box. We'd better not leave it behind. It's too precious to lose."

Reaching the Poet's Nook, she hastily removed the loose stone from the wall. George held it while Nancy reached inside.

"Hurry!" urged Bess, who was standing guard. "One of those men may come back any minute!"

Nancy retrieved the metal box, while George slid the stone back into place.

"Oh, please come!" Bess pleaded, and looked relieved when the others appeared.

Stealing noiselessly along, the three girls reached the castle. The door was unlocked! It made such a loud noise when they pulled it open that Nancy was fearful the sound would carry to the beach.

"What a weird place!" George commented, as they hurried inside and Nancy led the way along the winding corridor toward the front entrance.

"For all we know, we may be prisoners," Bess worried. "Let's get out of here as soon as we can."

Nancy, fairly familiar with the floor plan, found the main entrance. It was locked, but another door close by opened when she turned the knob.

"This is a break for us!" George exclaimed, going out first. She stepped onto a terrace, and there stopped short. "Oh! Oh!" she cried.

"Now what?" asked Nancy, closing the door.

Lying at the foot of the steps from the terrace were the two huge dogs the girls had met before. They began to growl menacingly.

"Well, hello, old fellows, we meet again!" Nancy said cheerily.

But her friendly attitude did not work this time. The animals would not allow the girls to descend the steps.

"You try it alone, Nancy," suggested Bess.

This was no better. The hounds were acting very strangely indeed.

"What can be wrong?" Nancy muttered, perplexed. "The other day these same dogs let me pass."

Nancy shifted the metal box under her arm and the dogs growled even more fiercely.

"Why, it's this box!" she realized. "They think I'm trying to steal something from the castle!"

Telling her friends she would return in a minute, Nancy ran back inside. It required but a minute to strip the box of the photographs and diary. Stuffing them beneath her sweater, she looked around.

"Where can I hide the box?" she thought. Suddenly her eyes caught sight of a door. "That closet will do," she told herself.

Darting across the big hall, she yanked open the door and placed the metal container on the floor. As she did so, the girl could hear footsteps not far away. Someone was coming along the winding corridor!

Nancy flew back to the terrace. The dogs growled but did not try to molest her this time. She hurried down the steps, her friends behind her. Bess was fearful, but tried not to show it.

"You girls go on ahead," ordered Nancy. "I'll keep the dogs busy until you get a good start. Then I'll follow."

Since there was no time to lose, they obeyed. Thirty seconds later, Nancy followed them.

The hounds set up a fearful barking as they leaped alongside the fleeing girl. The next minute Hector Keep's figure framed the doorway.

Nancy could not avoid being seen by him, although she covered her face with her free hand and kept on running.

"Hey, you!" the lawyer shouted furiously. "Stop! Stop!"

Nancy ignored his cries. Catching up with her friends, she urged them to a faster pace.

"Quick! The wall!" she panted, holding her treasure close inside her sweater.

Chapter XX

MEHEARTY'S PLIGHT

Closely pursued by the barking dogs, the three girls raced madly to the front wall of the estate. Scrambling safely over it, they paused, gasping for breath.

"What a narrow escape!" Nancy said shakily. "Hector Keep was after me!"

"Did he recognize you?" Bess asked her, worried.

"He doesn't really know me, and I kept my face covered as I ran."

"What did you do with the metal box?" Bess wanted to know.

"I hid it. But not these." Cautiously Nancy produced the photographs and the diary from beneath her sweater. "I still have the evidence!"

"You're wonderful," said George. "Well, what's next? We're a long way from the boat."

Having caught their breaths, the girls debated what to do. They were worried about Mehearty and what might have happened to him. Though the beach was not more than half a mile away, they had no way of reaching it.

"We'll have to return to town and rent another boat," Nancy concluded.

Walking as fast as they could, the trio made their way to the main highway. They were a long distance from River Heights, and Bess pointed out that bus service was infrequent along this route.

"Last time I was here I thought one never would come," she reminisced. "That wasn't very long ago, either, but it seems like a year to me!"

The girls waited patiently for twenty minutes, hoping a bus would appear. They were almost in despair, when Nancy observed a familiar coupé coming down the road.

"Lieutenant Masters' car!" she cried, holding up her hand in signal. "Now we'll get a ride."

The automobile came to a standstill at the side of the road. The young officer expressed delight at seeing Nancy and meeting her friends.

"Hop in," she invited them. "There isn't much room, but I think we all can squeeze in."

"Seeing you out here makes me think you've been to Heath Castle," the lieutenant said, a twinkle in her eye.

"We have been," Nancy admitted. "I suppose I ought to tell you everything, but——"

"But it's a professional secret. I understand," the attractive young officer laughed. "Tell me one thing, though. Is there any chance of your finding Florianna before it's too late?"

"I have several very good leads," the girl answered. "In fact, George and Bess and I were following one this morning. Mehearty came with us."

"Mehearty?"

"Yes. He's the singing clam digger of the Muskoka River. I'm sort of responsible for his nickname," Nancy explained. "He used to sing 'me hearty lad' and 'me hearty men', so when I was a little girl I called him Mehearty man."

"And now everyone in River Heights calls him Mehearty," said Bess. "The poor old fellow! We left him on the beach. He's probably in the hands of the crooks by now."

"What's that?" exclaimed the policewoman.

"Maybe I shouldn't have said that," Bess, remorseful, looked at Nancy.

The Drew girl explained as much as she felt to be necessary, and asked the officer if she thought a police boat might be sent out to rescue Mehearty.

"Why, of course!" Lieutenant Masters promised. "I'll call Headquarters as soon as we get to River Heights."

She remarked to Nancy that she had expected to stop at the Drew home to discuss the problem of Joan Fenimore and her playmate, Jeddy Hooker.

"She promised me she wouldn't play with Jeddy any more," said Nancy.

"I'm inclined to think she may have tried not to," the officer said slowly, "but—well, here's the story. Jeddy really causes me more worry than a dozen other boys on my list."

"What has he done this time?" Nancy asked curiously, though she thought she knew part of the answer already.

"He hasn't been in school for three days. It does no good to talk to his mother. I'm convinced she's an unsuitable person to look after him."

"I'll say she is," George burst out, and told Miss Masters about the clothes stolen from her, and how they suspected Jeddy and his mother of being in possession of them.

"I'm afraid the boy is a thief at heart," the lieutenant sighed. "Yesterday I caught him at Weatherby's curio shop trying to sell a fair-sized pearl."

"You think he stole it?" cried Nancy, thinking of the one taken from her.

"I'm not sure. When I took Jeddy home, his mother said she knew nothing about the pearl. Jeddy claimed that Joan Fenimore had given it to him, but Joan denied the story. So you see it's all very confusing."

"What a pity Joan has to be mixed up in such things!" said Nancy, shocked. "She's too nice a child."

"Jeddy's a very bad influence for her," the policewoman sighed. "Mrs. Fenimore realizes this only too well. She's willing to send the little girl away for a while if I can find a place for her to stay."

"That shouldn't be difficult," said Bess.

"I've had no luck so far, though I've made several inquiries. Nancy, do you know of anyone who would take the child?"

"I'll talk to our housekeeper about it," the Drew girl offered. "It's possible we can work out something. She has relatives who own a farm."

"That would be ideal for a while, since the child loves Nature," said the officer, as she stopped the coupé in front of the Drew home. "And now, if I may use your telephone, I'll call Headquarters and see about getting a boat to rescue that man Mehearty."

Lieutenant Masters called the police station, and talked with the sergeant on duty.

"The force is working shorthanded," she explained after putting down the receiver. "Only one man can go. Will you girls accompany him so that you can bring back the rented boat?"

"Yes, we'll be glad to," the three said together, and thanked the lieutenant for her help.

As it developed, Nancy was not to be included in the rescue party. She and her friends were about to leave the house when Mr. Drew drove up.

"Don't go away, Nancy!" he called urgently to his daughter. "I have something important to talk over with you."

"Do you mind if I don't go with you?" Nancy asked the other girls.

"No, not if there's a policeman along," Bess replied, and George nodded.

"Let me know what happens," Nancy requested, as the cousins went off with Lieutenant Masters. "I'm dreadfully anxious about Mehearty."

The woman drove Bess and George to the police dock and there said good-bye. Soon Policeman Carney arrived in a boat, and the girls climbed in. It was a fast craft, and reached the area of Heath Castle in a much shorter time than the one which Nancy had piloted.

To the girls' relief, the rented boat was still anchored in the river; but Mehearty was not in it. Nor was he or his rowboat visible on the beach.

"He wouldn't have had time to row home," said Bess, worried. "And we didn't pass him as we came up."

"Do you suppose those men——" whispered George grimly.

The girls told Policeman Carney they were afraid the old clam digger might have met with foul play and asked him to go ashore with them. He anchored his speedboat, and the three climbed into the rowboat it was hauling.

Reaching the beach, the searchers started an intensive hunt. They were just about to despair of finding the missing man, when George spied the form of the old sailor lying near the entrance to the cloister. For a moment she was fearful something dreadful had happened to him, but he suddenly sat up and looked at her.

"Thought ye'd never come," he muttered sleepily.

George thought he was only sleepy, until she noticed blood on his face and his shirt.

"Mehearty! You're hurt!" she exclaimed.

Her cry brought Bess and Policeman Carney leaping to her side. The old clam digger stood up and insisted he was all right, though he seemed somewhat unsteady.

"I'd be proud to get knocked out any time for Miss Nancy Drew," he murmured, "and nobody can say anything against her!" Mehearty looked around. "Where is she?" he demanded.

"Home," Bess replied.

"Home?" The man blinked. "How'd she get there? Not through here?" He pointed to the cloister opening.

"No. By the road," explained George. "Come, Mehearty, we'll go back to River Heights and talk on the way. Where's your boat?"

"Those rascals what give me a bloody nose took 'er," the old sailor explained.

Policeman Carney made sure the man was all right, then he said if the others did not mind, he would hurry back to River Heights alone. He waited long enough to be sure their boat started before speeding away.

"Now, Mehearty, tell us what happened," George demanded, as they skimmed down the stream toward Campbell's Landing.

"I was diggin' for clams," the old sailor began, "when a couple o' men and a boy seemed to come right out o' nowhere. They asked me who was in the Heath gardens."

"You didn't tell them!" Bess exclaimed.

"Yes, afore I thought I up and said, 'Nancy Drew and a couple of her friends.' It was a mistake to tell 'em. I learned that quick enough. Right away they told me to clear out, and said they'd go after the girls."

"What did you do then?" George asked.

"I tried to argue 'em out of it, but they was stubborn as mules. Then one of 'em said something about Miss Nancy bein' dangerous and she'd better mind her own business. I up and punched him on the nose for that."

"You were nice to come to Nancy's defence," said Bess, "but there were three against you."

"Ye're right, and we had a tussle. 'Fraid I lost the battle," the clam digger added sheepishly. "But I come to pretty soon; in fact, just in time to see one o' them rascals takin' my boat."

Mehearty told how he had noticed one of the other men going through the section of wall with the stone steps beyond and decided to follow him. But the poor old sailor had got no farther than the opening, before everything went black before him.

"Later I come to," he said, "but I couldn't seem to move for a while. Somewhere in the garden I heard two men talkin'. I'm glad Miss Nancy is home safe, for one of 'em said he was goin' to have her arrested!"

"Arrested!" cried Bess. "Why?"

"I didn't hear. I guess I must have kind of gone off again," the old man replied.

"We must warn Nancy right away!" George declared, pushing the boat to its utmost speed.

Unaware that her chums were racing to caution her of trouble, Nancy in the meantime had been eating a late luncheon and talking with her father at home. Eagerly she showed him the photographs and diary she had removed from the metal box. She spoke of the mysterious Cinderella footprint embedded in the crumbling wall at the Heath gardens, and gave a vivid account of her adventure with Cobb, Biggs, and Hector Keep.

"You certainly had no dull moments," Mr. Drew commented. "Your news dwarfs what I have to tell you."

"Is it something that will help solve the mystery?" Nancy asked eagerly.

"It may, depending upon how you use the information."

The girl squirmed impatiently. "Don't keep me in suspense," she pleaded. "What is the news, Dad?"

"It concerns Florianna's missing nurse."

"Emily Foster?"

"Yes," Mr. Drew nodded. "After a long search, I've located her. And here's the best part of it all. Tomorrow morning she'll be glad to see you and tell you all she knows!"

Chapter XXI

NEWS OF FLORIANNA

"Oh, Dad! Where *is* Emily Foster?" Nancy cried, thrilled by the wonderful news. "How did you find her? What did she say about Florianna?"

"One question at a time," laughed Mr. Drew. "I talked with Miss Foster only by telephone, so I did not get any details."

"Is she here in River Heights?"

"No, I traced her by contacting various nurses' registries. Miss Foster is working on a case at Hampton. She'll be free tomorrow, and has promised to meet us at the hotel there."

"Then we're both going to Hampton?"

"If you care to go with me, Nancy. I must drive over on business anyway."

"If I care to!" Nancy said feelingly. "This is the chance of a lifetime! Oh, Dad, wouldn't it be wonderful if we could find Florianna tomorrow?"

"Don't build your hopes too high," the lawyer warned his daughter kindly. "Miss Foster may not know what became of the dancer. Even if she is able to provide a clue, the time is very short for you to follow it up."

"That's the trouble," Nancy agreed, worried. "Only a few

days are left before Heath Castle will be turned over to the county."

"Anyway, it seems to me you've built up a case against Hector Keep, and that's something," her father said in praise of her work. "Even if Florianna is never found, there's no reason why that unscrupulous lawyer and his henchmen should help themselves to any of the estate."

The Drews planned to leave for Hampton that afternoon and spend the night at a hotel in order to be there early in the morning. Knowing she had a dozen things to do before leaving, Nancy fairly flew to the tasks.

Her first act was to consult Hannah Gruen about little Joan Fenimore. The housekeeper immediately telephoned her relative, Mrs. Davis, at her farm. The woman said she would be happy indeed to take the child for a visit. Nancy then notified Lieutenant Masters, but the policewoman was so busy she said it would be impossible for her to see Mrs. Fenimore that day. As a favour, she asked the girl to go in her stead.

"All right, I'll be glad to," Nancy said, though she wondered how she would find the time.

Mr. Drew, knowing that his daughter had more than enough to do, generously offered to assist. He dropped into the police station and related to the Chief what Nancy had seen and heard that day at Heath Castle. He asked that a search be made for the two men, Biggs and Cobb.

"We'll pick them up," the officer promised. "But without more evidence we'll not be able to hold 'em very long."

"By that time, maybe my daughter or I will have further evidence for you," the lawyer smiled.

When Mr. Drew returned home, Nancy was ready to leave. She suggested they stop at the Fenimore cottage to extend the invitation for Joan to visit at the Davis farm. To her surprise she found the invalid in very good spirits.

"The Hooker family has moved away!" she disclosed as the cause of her jubilation. "Now Joan and Jeddy will be separated. It won't be necessary for me to send my little girl away for a visit."

Nancy glanced at her father. He shook his head, indi-
cating that it would be wise to forget the arrangement just
made with Mrs. Davis.

"I wonder why your neighbours left so suddenly?" Nancy
mused.

"It was strange," Mrs. Fenimore replied. "Mrs. Hooker
never talked about leaving. Around noon today a truck
drove up with Mr. Hooker and another man. They loaded
a lot of furniture in it. Then Mrs. Hooker and Jeddy left in
a taxi with their bags."

Mrs. Fenimore went on to say that Jeddy had been boast-
ing to Joan lately.

"He said his father was a smart man—that he knew how
to make money without working for it. Oh, the talk frightened me."

"I've never seen Mr. Hooker," Nancy said, extremely interested in the remark. "Can you describe him?"

"Cobb Hooker is a tall man, sullen-faced, and unkempt
in appearance."

"Did you say Cobb Hooker!" Nancy exclaimed, startled
by the name.

"Yes."

Nancy let the matter pass without comment, but asked
Mrs. Fenimore if there was anything more she could tell her
about Jeddy and his family.

"I never knew when that boy was telling the truth," the
invalid replied. "But he told Joan that he knew where there
was a hidden treasure."

"Hidden treasure!" Nancy echoed, light dawning upon
her. "Mrs. Fenimore, did Joan ever talk to the Hookers
about Florianna and the property she was to inherit?"

"Dear me, yes! The child told everybody about it. The
story became almost an obsession with her."

"And Jeddy repeated the tale to his parents?" commented
Mr. Drew.

"I don't know. But Jeddy told Joan he'd gone to Heath
Castle himself. He threatened her if she told anyone about
it."

The Drews made no comment about this. Soon they got up to leave, saying they were on their way to interview a woman who might give them some information about Florianna.

"Oh, I hope she can!" cried Mrs. Fenimore eagerly.

As soon as Nancy and her father left the cottage, the girl told him of her suspicion regarding Cobb Hooker.

"Until now I assumed that Cobb was a last name," she commented. "It never occurred to me that Biggs' companion might be Jeddy's father!"

"You're not sure of it now, Nancy."

"True. But Cobb is not a common name. Shouldn't we talk to the police again? Unwittingly I've given them the wrong information."

Mr. Drew glanced at his watch. "Very well," he consented. "But we've not much time if we're to get to Hampton tonight."

The call at the local police station did not take long, and proved to be of great value. Cobb Hooker, the Chief informed the Drews after consulting some records, had a police record. Three years before he had served a term on a burglary charge in a distant town.

"Have you a picture of the man?" Mr. Drew asked.

The photograph was brought from the files. One glance at it told Nancy that at last she knew the identity of the man who had run into her with his boat.

"And Cobb Hooker is one of the men who was in the Heath gardens," she revealed.

"If you'll make a formal charge against the fellow, we'll try to track him down and arrest him," offered the Chief.

Mr. Drew did not wish to be too hasty. "Couldn't we learn more by having one of your men trail him for a few days?" he suggested.

"That's a good idea. I'll put someone on the case right away, Mr. Drew," said the officer, and turned to answer his telephone.

Two hours after Nancy and her father had left town, Bess and George, highly excited, arrived at the Drew house.

E

Upon hearing from Hannah Gruen that their friend had gone away, the girls looked relieved.

"Is anything the matter?" asked the housekeeper.

"Plenty. Somebody is going to have Nancy arrested."

"Who?"

"We don't know. Mehearty heard about it."

It was well that Mrs. Gruen had been warned what to expect, because that very evening a policeman came to the door with a warrant for Nancy's arrest.

"Miss Drew isn't here," the housekeeper said, thoroughly enjoying the situation. "I don't know when she'll be back, either. Perhaps not for some time."

"You have her address?"

"No, I haven't. She and her father went off in a hurry. They didn't leave any address."

"You're trying to protect the girl!" the officer said. "Oh, well, it's nothing to me one way or the other. I was told to serve this warrant. If she's not here, I can't do it."

Temporarily safe from arrest, Nancy arrived at the Hampton Hotel with her father. The next morning they waited expectantly for Emily Foster to call. At ten o'clock, the time set for the appointment, the nurse had not arrived. Both Mr. Drew and his daughter became anxious lest their trip end in failure. Then fifteen minutes later, the woman came hurrying into the lobby.

"I'm sorry to be late," she apologized breathlessly, as Nancy advanced to meet her, "but the nurse who was to relieve me didn't come on time."

Nancy and her father liked Miss Foster at once. She was a woman of early middle age, brisk and efficient, with a friendly smile.

"Mr. Drew, you said over the telephone that you and your daughter wanted to ask me about a former patient of mine," she began at once. "I'll be glad to answer any questions I can."

"As I explained, we're seeking information about a certain Flossie Johnson. The young woman also used the name of Florianna," said the lawyer.

"I never took care of anyone who called herself by either of those names. The patient you asked me about—a beautiful young woman injured in an automobile accident about ten years ago—gave her name as Miss Flower."

"Tell us about her," Mr. Drew urged. "From the facts we've already gathered, it seems fairly evident that she is the one for whom we're looking."

"She was a hospital case, assigned to me about ten years ago," Miss Foster recalled. "The girl interested me more than the average patient. She was so beautiful, so unassuming, and yet so distinguished. From the first, I felt that she had not registered under her real name."

"What made you think so?" Mr. Drew inquired.

"Mostly little remarks she dropped. One peculiar thing was that Miss Flower never had visitors. No messages came for her. There were no letters. She would allow the authorities to notify no one of the accident. 'I don't want anyone to know,' she would say. 'Not until I'm well.'"

"The young woman believed she would recover completely?" Nancy asked quickly.

"Only the first few weeks. Then the doctor told her the truth—that she would be a cripple for the rest of her life."

"How did she take it?" Mr. Drew questioned.

"Very hard. She wept for days, saying the strangest things. One remark I recall was, 'His little Cinderella never will dance for him again.' Oh, it was heartbreaking to listen to her."

Cinderella!

Nancy was so sure now she was on the right track that her mind leaped from one possibility to another. She nearly missed her father's next question.

"Where did the girl go after she left the hospital?"

"I never heard," Miss Foster admitted regretfully. "From Miss Flower's remarks, I assumed that she intended to retire to some secluded place near Hopewell."

"Yet it's unlikely the woman had much money with her," Mr. Drew commented. "When she was picked up, I understand no purse was found."

"That's true," said the nurse, "but she had some money in her possession, though she couldn't have had much left after she paid her hospital bill."

"All these years she must have earned a living somehow," commented Nancy. "You have no idea how, of course?"

"No, I haven't."

"That name Flower," Nancy mused. "Florianna was deeply interested in gardening," she added, recalling what Mrs. Fenimore had told her about the dancer.

"And so was Miss Flower!" the nurse exclaimed. "She was always asking me to buy her garden magazines. Why, the day before her release, I remember she cut an advertisement from the local paper——"

"Yes?" Nancy asked eagerly as the nurse hesitated.

"Probably it has no significance," Miss Foster completed. "But the advertisement Miss Flower clipped out offered a small fruit and vegetable farm for sale—a place known as Clover Farm."

"Where is the farm?" Nancy asked, her eyes dancing with hope.

"It seems to me there's a Clover Farm at Hilton about ten miles from here. I don't know whether it's the same one, though."

Nancy turned to her father.

"Yes, we'll go there today!" he said, reading his daughter's thoughts. "It may be a vain chase, but something tells me that this time we'll find Florianna!"

Chapter XXII

THE RECLUSE OF CLOVER FARM

AFTER bidding Miss Foster good-bye, Nancy and her father drove directly to Hilton. Inquiry at the little village revealed that Clover Farm was well-known and famous for its superb fruits and vegetables. Yet strangely enough, no one could tell the Drews anything about the owner.

"Fact is, folks hereabouts never lay eyes on Miss Flower," a filling station attendant explained to them. "She bought the place ten years ago. To my knowledge, she's never set foot off the farm since."

"Then how does she market her products?" Mr. Drew asked.

"Sends her farmhands to town with the vegetables. All her help has been with her for years. They're a loyal lot, and she's taught 'em to be close-mouthed."

Mr. Drew inquired how to reach the farm. He was instructed to drive on for two and a half miles before turning into a private side road.

"You'll see a big sign reading 'Clover Farm, No Visitors Admitted,'" the filling station man added. "It means what it says, too!"

Convinced that at last they were nearing the end of a long search, Nancy and her father drove on in high spirits. Presently they came to the sign the man had mentioned. A decorative wooden gate, flanked by tall hedges, barred admittance to the farm.

With assurance, Mr. Drew opened the gate and drove up the winding lane. Nancy glimpsed a small, white clapboard house surrounded by flower beds. There was an orchard, and two large fields of vegetables. Suddenly two men in overalls leaped out from the roadside. Mr. Drew was forced to bring the car to a halt.

"No visitors allowed here!" one of the farmhands said curtly. "Can't you read signs?"

"We came to see the owner of Clover Farm," Mr. Drew explained. "Our business with her is urgent."

"Did Miss Flower send for you?"

"No," Mr. Drew admitted, "but we have important information for Miss Flower."

The workmen hesitated. Then one of them said impatiently, "Sorry. You can't see her."

Disgusted, Mr. Drew was ready to go on to the house

despite them. Nancy made a last desperate attempt to gain their co-operation.

"You'll be doing Miss Flower a favour if you'll let us talk to her," she pleaded. "You see, your employer has inherited a fortune. But she must claim it within the next few days or she'll lose it."

The men's jaws dropped.

"Is that the truth?" one of them demanded.

"Certainly," snapped Mr. Drew. "Now will you tell Miss Flower we'd like to see her?"

"She's not here."

Nancy and her father were dumbfounded.

"But we've been told Miss Flower never leaves Clover Farm!" the girl protested.

"She never did until last night on account of being such a cripple. But when that government man came for her, she had to go. He took her away in a car."

"What government man?" Mr. Drew asked quickly. "Did he give his name?"

"He prob'ly told Miss Flower. We didn't hear it. Fact is, we didn't see her go. She left a note."

"Did she say why she had to go with him?" asked Nancy.

"It was something about income tax. Miss Flower always thought she paid the government every penny she owed. She's as honest as the day is long. But the man claimed she'd made a false report and might have to go to prison."

"This seems very irregular to me," commented Mr. Drew. "Assuming that Miss Flower made a mistake in the amount of her tax, she could not be sentenced without a hearing. The usual procedure would be to notify her by letter and have her call at the tax office to explain her side of the matter."

"Dad," Nancy said, looking anxiously at him, "it looks as if someone was very eager to get Miss Flower away from here!"

"Before we found her, you mean?"

"Yes. Oh, Dad, we must do something!"

"First of all, we'll check with the revenue office; that is, if I can get to a telephone."

The two farmhands, sensing that Nancy and her father were sincere, invited them into the farmhouse. Mr. Drew busied himself at the telephone, while Nancy looked at the note Miss Flower had left. The writing showed such haste and nervousness she could not identify it as Florianna's.

The telephone call required a few minutes. When the lawyer finished it, he looked grim.

"Just as we feared," he revealed. "The Federal Bureau has no case pending against Miss Flower."

"Then it was all a hoax!"

"Yes. The man who came here was an impostor. Obviously, it was a scheme to get her away from Clover Farm."

The news of what had befallen the owner spread to Miss Flower's other two employees who were in the fields. They came in, their faces sad. The woman was loved and respected by them, and it was feared that she would suffer at the hands of her captor.

"I wouldn't worry on that score," Mr. Drew said to comfort the men. "Miss Flower probably will receive good treatment. But unfortunately, she will lose a fortune unless she can be found within a week."

The farmhands looked to the Drews to do something about the matter. Nancy and her father promised to stop at the police station and report the kidnapping. The description the men of Clover Farm gave of the stranger was not very helpful—he was tall, slightly stooped, wore dark glasses, and had a beard.

"Probably a disguise," Nancy concluded.

After telling their story to the local police, the Drews returned to the Hampton Hotel. Both Nancy and her father were discouraged.

And still another surprise in the case awaited them!

On his way to the dining room to luncheon, Carson Drew purchased a copy of the River Heights afternoon newspaper. A startling headline caught his eye. He gasped when he read it.

"What is it?" cried Nancy.

Her father thrust the paper before her, pointing to the item.

FAMOUS DANCER
RETURNS IN TIME TO
CLAIM HEATH FORTUNE

The story which followed stated that after a long search, Hector Keep had found the missing Florianna, who now was staying at the local Riverview Hotel. For many years the famous dancer had been abroad fulfilling professional engagements.

"Then she isn't Miss Flower!" said Nancy, her hopes tumbling.

Florianna had married a South American dancer, José Fernandez, and had been difficult to trace because she had used her husband's name. Hector Keep was given high praise for having found the woman in time to prevent her from losing the Heath fortune.

Nancy's discouragement lasted only a moment. Then her old suspicions returned. "This can't be true!" she fairly wailed. "It must be a scheme to give the estate to an impostor—an accomplice of Mr. Keep's!"

"There's something underhanded about it!" Mr. Drew agreed, his face grim.

"Let's hurry back to River Heights and learn what we can!" Nancy begged.

Hastening through the meal, she and her father checked out of the hotel. They were convinced that Hector Keep had produced someone who resembled the missing Florianna. If he were able to establish her as the heiress, undoubtedly he would pay her well and then take over the estate for himself.

"Poor little Miss Flower!" Nancy said sadly, as the car sped along the road. "I'm sure she's Florianna! Oh, where have they hidden her?"

It was late afternoon by the time the Drews reached River Heights. Mr. Drew said he had to stop at his office to attend to some matters for a couple of hours, and that Nancy should take the car to do her investigating.

"I believe I'll stop in to see Mrs. Fenimore and find out if she has heard the news," the girl decided, turning the automobile in the direction of the little cottage.

The invalid and Joan were preparing supper when Nancy arrived. The child at once invited Nancy to eat with them, but the Drew girl shook her head, plunging at once into the subject uppermost in her mind. The Fenimores had not heard the exciting announcement.

"My darling sister has been found!" the widow cried, not realizing that the claimant might be an impostor. "Oh, why hasn't she come to see me? Please take me to her at once!"

All thought of supper was forgotten by the woman and her young daughter. Joan insisted upon going along to see her famous aunt. Hurriedly they changed into their best clothes and rode with Nancy to the Riverview Hotel.

"Madam Fernandez?" the clerk at the desk repeated when Nancy inquired for the woman. "I'll see if she's receiving callers. I believe she's having dinner in her room."

While the little group waited, Mrs. Fenimore became so nervous that she could hardly control herself. She began to feel faint, and Nancy brought her a glass of water.

"I wonder if Florianna has changed much," she speculated, adjusting her hat for the hundredth time. "Imagine her marrying a foreigner! Florianna always used to say she never would marry anyone except an American."

Twenty minutes elapsed. Then word was sent to the callers that they might go up to Room Thirty-two. When they knocked a few minutes later, a voice said:

"Come in!"

Florianna Fernandez was reclining on the bed, her back braced by several embroidered pillows. She wore an exotic negligee which set off to advantage her dark hair and creamy white skin.

"Greetings, my dear sister," she said as the three entered. She spoke in a stiff, affected way, as if English were difficult for her. "Vera, I am so glad to see you again! This so charming child, she is Joan, of course. And this lovely señorita?"

Mrs. Fenimore was so confused that for an instant she

could not speak. Joan clung to her mother. Nancy filled in the breach by giving her name.

"Miss Drew?" The dancer looked perplexed, but only for an instant. "Yes, I believe my dear friend Señor Keep tell me you are a friend of Vera." Turning to Mrs. Fenimore, she added, "Oh, I am so happy Señor Keep found me!"

"Florianna, you've changed," Mrs. Fenimore stammered. Going hesitantly to the bed, she would have kissed the dancer. The woman, however, drew back quickly as if she dreaded an embrace.

"I am a famous dancer now!" Florianna said proudly. "And you should see my husband—one of the best dancers in South America! But it is hard work. We shall return to our home with much gold in our pockets, and work no more!"

The meeting was going very badly indeed. Mrs. Fenimore was so stunned by the change in her sister that she could find nothing to say. Joan too merely opened her eyes wide and kept still. Nancy sought to keep the conversational ball rolling, for she was becoming more suspicious of the woman by the minute.

"Suppose you tell us what you've been doing all these years," she encouraged the dancer. "I notice that English seems a bit difficult for you."

"That is because I have lived so long in South America. For ten years I speak almost no English—only *Español*."

"Then you went there immediately after you gave up your career here?"

"*Si*, I elope with darling husband."

"But how could you desert Walter Heath?" Mrs. Fenimore murmured. "He was so good to you—so kind."

"I could not marry Walt when I did not love him—no! To save him much hurt, I ran away."

"And now you return to claim the Heath fortune," Nancy interposed, disgusted at such a procedure.

"*Si, si!* Señor Keep tell me that I will be rich heiress!"

"I suppose you and your husband will restore the gardens and make the estate a show place again," the Drew girl suggested.

Florianna's pretty face clouded. "No, we do not plan so," she replied firmly. "Señor Keep will sell the castle for us. He has a buyer now, he tell me."

"But, Florianna!" Mrs. Fenimore protested faintly. "Surely you will remain in River Heights! At least for a time. Joan and I need you."

"I have my career—a great star cannot be tied to her family. It grows late. You will excuse me now. We will meet again, Vera darling."

Deeply hurt at being so curtly dismissed, Mrs. Fenimore moved slowly to the door, her head bowed. There she paused, the picture of dejection.

"Your hair, Florianna," she said, turning to the glamorous woman. "When last I saw it——"

"I dye it black to look more like the Spanish señorita," the dancer said quickly.

Nancy was firmly convinced from the woman's contradictory remarks that Madam Fernandez was an impostor, but she dared not say so. She did have the courage, however, to ask Florianna what proof she would be able to produce to establish her claim to the Heath fortune.

"Señor Keep have all the papers," the dancer said glibly. "If anyone doubt me, let him read this!"

From beneath her pillow Florianna brought forth a torn paper. Nancy instantly knew that it was the missing half of the note she had found at the Heath Factory! She read the words:

> day the se-
> am hiding
> will make me
> Then I shall be
> of you. Love,
> Walt.

Nancy did not have the other half of the note with her, but she knew its contents by heart. The complete message would read:

Dear C,
Some day the se-
cret which I am hiding
in a wall will make me
famous. Then I shall be
worthy of you. Love,
Walt.

It seemed to the girl that here was proof Walter Heath had not sold nor used the valuable whelk dye on which he had experimented. Instead, he had hidden it somewhere in the old estate walls until he should have perfected his work. Florianna meanwhile had become successful. He had hoped to attain a name for himself as a scientist and thus feel he was worthy of her.

"You haven't the other half of the note?" Nancy asked, returning the paper to the dancer.

"No, I lose it years ago. I do not remember what it say."

"By the way, did Walter Heath have a pet name for you—a nickname?" the girl inquired.

"Oh, *sí,*" the woman replied glibly. "He call me Precious."

"No particular name?"

"I do not understand what you mean."

"Never mind," said Nancy, well pleased by the reply. "It doesn't make any difference."

She followed Mrs. Fenimore and Joan from the room. Once outside, the child said bluntly:

"I don't like my new aunt."

"Sh, she may hear you," her mother warned.

When the callers were seated in the car again, Nancy asked the widow if she were convinced Mrs. Fernandez was her sister.

"I don't know, I don't know," the poor woman replied, weeping. "Florianna is so changed. In some ways she resembles my sister; her height and weight, the tone of her voice—yes, even her face. But the black hair makes her look different, of course."

"In other words, you couldn't say after ten years that she is *not* your sister?"

"No, I'm afraid I couldn't," Vera Fenimore admitted.

"Then if she is an impostor, Hector Keep has done a good job," Nancy told herself. "I'll have to produce expert evidence to outwit him." Aloud she said, "I noticed that Mrs. Fernandez had rather large feet. Her slippers must be size eight at least."

"Florianna had extremely small feet!" exclaimed Mrs. Fenimore.

"So I thought," Nancy said. "I doubt that they would have changed so much."

"Then the woman is not my sister!"

"I'm afraid not. That's why she's unwilling to help you and Joan."

"Can't we expose her?"

"I'm going to try," Nancy said grimly. "But doing so won't restore your real sister to you. I still must find her."

"Didn't you learn anything on your trip?" the widow asked. "You hinted——"

Nancy did not have the heart to tell the distracted woman any more bad news. She merely mentioned having interviewed someone who thought she had met Florianna under an assumed name.

"I'll go right on working to find your sister until the last minute," Nancy promised.

"Please don't ever stop," begged Vera Fenimore pathetically. "If Flossie doesn't inherit the estate, she doesn't, that's all. But if she's alive, I want to see her again, no matter when it may be."

"I'll try to accomplish both things," were Nancy's parting words, as she left Joan and her mother at their cottage.

Deep in thought, Nancy drove toward home. As she neared the police station, she suddenly decided to drop in and get a report on Cobb and Biggs. Unaware that contacting the police was exactly what Hector Keep wanted her to do, Nancy innocently walked into the main room at Headquarters.

"Miss Drew!" exclaimed the sergeant on duty at the desk. "You're the very person we've been looking for! We have a warrant for your arrest!"

Chapter XXIII

IN THE DUNGEON

NANCY was stunned at the sergeant's words.

"Under arrest?" she gasped. "What for?"

The officer opened a drawer and took out the summons which he read aloud. Nancy learned that she was charged with illegal entry into the Heath estate, as well as damage to property and stealing.

"Who preferred the charges?" the girl asked, unable to believe what she had just heard.

"Mr. Hector Keep."

"Oh!"

Nancy indignantly denied all charges save one. She readily admitted she had disobeyed a No Trespassing sign, but felt she had a legitimate reason for doing so.

"Lieutenant Masters can explain everything," she insisted. "Please ask her to come here. And I'd like to get in touch with my father, too."

Mr. Drew arrived shortly, followed by the young police-woman. He consulted privately with her, Captain Walker, and the Chief of Police. Nancy then was called in to tell her story. Eloquently she spoke of what she had seen and heard at Heath Castle. She mentioned her suspicion regarding Keep's association with the two men, Biggs and Cobb, who, she learned, were still at large. The girl concluded by saying that she thought Keep made the charges against her to prevent her from working on the case.

"There's something to what you say," the Chief agreed. "Well, if Mr. Keep will let me tear up these complaint papers, I'll call everything off."

But the wily lawyer could not be located, so the warrant remained intact. In the end Nancy was allowed to go home with a promise on her part that she would come back to Headquarters the following morning.

She and her father talked until midnight, then Mr. Drew insisted his daughter get some rest. Obediently the girl went to bed, but she could not sleep. The day's happenings had been too exciting. Hour after hour Nancy struggled to fit together the pieces of the crazy puzzle. Several times she thought she had the problem solved, but one item kept eluding her.

"Hector Keep wanted me arrested to hinder me from going to Heath Castle. But why? Surely not because of anything I've seen there already. Is it because of something else hidden on the place?"

The girl felt sure there was something more to it than this. Suddenly she was sure she had the answer. She could hardly wait now to get back to the police station!

Tiptoeing downstairs early the next morning before the others in the house were awake, she ate her breakfast, wrote a note to her father, and left for Headquarters. The day sergeant was just coming on duty. He grinned at her, saying that she need not have reported so soon, that she hardly looked rested.

"I didn't sleep a wink last night," Nancy admitted, "but I did get some ideas. As soon as Lieutenant Masters comes, I wish she might go out with me for a little while."

The officer said he felt sure this could be arranged. When the young policewoman came in, the girl repeated her request.

"Miss Masters, will you go to Heath Castle with me? I have a hunch the mystery will be solved there this morning!"

At Nancy's instigation several policemen were detailed to station themselves outside the Heath gardens to question anyone entering or leaving the grounds. The girl left at once with the lieutenant, and the men followed in another car.

"Just what do you expect to find at the castle?" the young woman asked Nancy curiously.

"It's my opinion that Hector Keep or one of his men kidnapped the real Florianna," Nancy disclosed to her companion. "He'll hold her until Madam Fernandez can establish her claim to the fortune. Keep will take the lion's share of it and then he'll disappear."

"But what has Heath Castle to do with it?" Lieutenant Masters asked. "You don't think Florianna is being imprisoned there?"

"That's my theory. Maybe it's just fancy, but it's the only reason I can think of why Hector Keep went to such lengths to have me arrested. He found out I was hot on the trail of Miss Flower, the real Florianna, and he had to get her out of the way. What better hiding place for his prisoner than the castle? Then, of course, he'd have to prevent me from trespassing there any more, so he cooked up the story you heard."

"Your reasoning certainly is logical," her companion admitted. "The crippled woman easily could have been brought to the place at night. Locked in one of those towers, she would be quite helpless."

"What worries me is whether we can get in," said Nancy after she and the policewoman had climbed the wall and set out for the castle. "I'm glad those dogs are gone, anyway."

"If necessary, we can force a lock," Lieutenant Masters assured her. "You have the Law at your side," she smiled.

Reassured, Nancy led the way to the front entrance. To her surprise, it stood ajar.

"Hector Keep may be here," she whispered guardedly. "Or perhaps Cobb, and possibly Biggs."

There was a not a sign of anyone stirring about the premises. Noiselessly, Nancy and the policewoman slipped inside the castle. Hearing no one, they tiptoed along the winding corridor to the courtyard garden where the entrances to the towers were. Nancy tried the door of the one in which she had been imprisoned. It was not locked.

"Will you stand guard while I go upstairs?" Nancy asked the policewoman quietly.

The other nodded, and the girl noiselessly ascended the circular iron staircase. She was gone several minutes, and Lieutenant Masters was just becoming uneasy about her when Nancy reappeared.

"No one there," she reported. "I looked over the grounds, too, but I didn't see anything suspicious."

"What's next?" asked the officer.

"There's a trap door," Nancy revealed, pointing toward the floor. "What it opens into I haven't been able to find out."

To raise it was indeed a task, but together they finally got it up. Cautiously Nancy and Lieutenant Masters peered into the darkness below.

The policewoman snapped on a flashlight, and they could see a flight of iron steps leading down into a long corridor. Grilled doors opened from it.

"It looks like a series of dungeons!" Nancy exclaimed. "A regular old-time prison!"

"Anyone below?" Lieutenant Masters called.

There was no answer, though her voice echoed weirdly. Then Nancy thought she heard a sound like a moan. She and the young woman scurried down the stairway.

Lieutenant Masters flashed her light into the first cell. It was a tiny room, musty and dark. The only bit of sunlight visible filtered in through a high, barred window.

"These rooms must have been built to imitate the old dungeons in the original castle," Nancy commented.

"No doubt the Heaths used them for storing food," the lieutenant said.

The next two rooms also were empty. But as Nancy and the policewoman approached the third, they distinctly heard someone moan. Pausing to listen intently, they caught a pitiful cry from the far end of the corridor:

"Let me out! Let me out! Please help me!"

Nancy and the young officer sped up the passageway. A small woman, crippled and weak, had pulled herself to the grilled doorway. She clung there, her eyes eloquent and beseeching.

"You're Florianna!" Nancy said quickly.

"No! No!" The prisoner shrank back. "I am Miss Flower."

"We'll talk about that later."

Nancy unbolted the door. She and Lieutenant Masters assisted the woman along the musty corridor, but it was slow work, for she had to pause often.

"Who brought you here?" the policewoman asked her kindly. "And have you been mistreated?"

"I've had enough to eat and drink," Miss Flower said. "But I've been so perplexed."

Questioned by Nancy and Miss Masters, she revealed all that had befallen her. An elderly man, who had shown an identification card of a government agent, had taken her away from Clover Farm in an automobile. It was dark when they reached their destination. She had been hurried inside a dimly lighted building and locked in the cell.

"I was told it was because of not paying enough income tax," she ended the story. "What does it all mean?"

"A great deal has happened since you left your home ten years ago," Nancy said.

"I—I don't know what you're talking about!"

"You are Florianna," Nancy said with quiet conviction. "Why not admit it?"

"No, no, never!"

"Do you realize where you are now?" Nancy asked, taking a different tack.

"It was dark when they brought me here. I could distinguish nothing."

"You are at Heath Castle."

"Heath Castle! You mean—Walt——?"

"Walter Heath died a number of years ago," Nancy said gently. "He loved you to the end and willed all his property to you."

"Walt—dead!" the woman whispered. "Then to the very end he thought of me as I used to be—beautiful, and a talented dancer."

"He thought of you as you still are," the policewoman spoke up. "A beautiful character with great charm."

Florianna brushed a wisp of straggling gold-grey hair from her eyes. Her slumping shoulders stiffened.

"But these withered, ugly legs!" she cried out. "Oh, I

want to be left alone with my sorrows. I have my little farm. Take me back there, please."

"You mean you don't want Heath Castle?" asked Lieutenant Masters.

"I loved Heath Castle, and I loved Walt," Florianna said brokenly. "But I hid myself away so that he never would see me as a cripple. Perhaps it is foolish pride, but it seems best that I finish out my days as I am doing."

"Your sister Vera wants to see you very much," said Nancy. "She is a widow now with a little girl who looks a great deal like you."

For the first time, Florianna was deeply moved. "Vera has a little girl?" she murmured. "Where is she?"

"She and her mother, Mrs. Fenimore, live in River Heights. The child's name is Joan. She likes flowers and gardening just as you do. I can't tell you the whole story now, but they need your help."

"If I had known before——" Florianna began.

"You were too proud to write to your sister?"

"Yes, at the beginning. Then later a letter I sent to her came back. I had no idea where she was."

"Mrs. Fenimore and Joan want to leave the neighbourhood where they live. Joan would be so happy in the gardens here," Lieutenant Masters said.

"Are the gardens still beautiful?" the former dancer asked dreamily.

Nancy hated to tell the woman the truth. She tried to soften it by saying, "They have been badly neglected. But they could be re-planted. Only one who truly loved the place, though, would want to do it."

"To me it would be a challenge," Florianna said with sudden spirit. "A memorial to Walt."

She added that the castle and its grounds really were pretty large for only three people.

"What a wonderful spot it would be for underprivileged children," the policewoman mused. "River Heights always has needed just such a place, especially for its crippled youngsters."

"I'd like to help them too!" Florianna announced
excitedly. "Yes, I'll build this place into a beauty spot
again! I'll bring Joan and Vera here. And later we'll see
about the others."

"Good!" approved Nancy. "We'll take you right to your
sister, and then I'll go to settle my score with Mr. Hector
Keep!"

The trio had reached the foot of the stairway. Before the
crippled woman could be helped up the steps, there came a
disturbing sound from overhead.

The next instant the trap door dropped into place. As the
bolt clicked, a voice reached their ears.

"That'll hold you! Try to get out now!"

The footsteps died away. Then all was quiet in the
dungeon.

Chapter XXIV

KEEP'S FINAL TRIUMPH

Nancy darted up the stairway to test the trap door. As she
had feared, it was locked.

"We're prisoners!" she exclaimed. "Hector Keep or one of
his men must have heard us!"

Lieutenant Masters was even more worried than Nancy,
but she said calmly:

"I feel sure there's no cause for alarm. Anyone trying to
leave the grounds will be captured by police guards. And
when we fail to show up, help will come."

"But will the trap door be noticed by anyone?" Nancy
asked dubiously. Then hopefully she added, "Perhaps I can
find another exit."

While Lieutenant Masters remained with Florianna, she
searched the various cells. No exit could be found. The only

openings were the high grilled windows. Nancy carried her discouraging report to the young officer.

"Miss Masters, have you a police whistle?" she asked, struck by a sudden idea.

The woman nodded. "Yes, and a gun, too."

"Then maybe we can get out of here! By standing on my shoulders, you should be able to reach one of the windows and signal for help."

Leaving Florianna sitting on the steps, Nancy and the policewoman stepped into the nearest cell. Lieutenant Masters was not a heavy woman. By standing on Nancy's shoulders, she reached the window, partially supporting herself by clinging to the iron grills. She blew a dozen shrill blasts with the police whistle.

"Hope that'll work," the officer said. "If not, I'll try firing a few shots."

She dropped lightly to the floor, wondering how long they might have to wait. Neither she nor Nancy was confident of being found soon; in fact, they were very worried about the little lady whom they had rescued, and who again had become a prisoner, together with themselves. How long could she stand the added strain?

Nancy sat down on the steps beside her to wait. Florianna was far from talkative, but the girl gradually drew her out. One of the first questions Nancy asked her was whether Walter Heath had given her a large pearl.

"No, but he was going to. It was being made into a ring when I went away."

Nancy next inquired if her fiancé had had a special name for her.

"Yes, he called me his little Cinderella," Florianna said, smiling at the recollection. "Once Walt asked me to step into a block of newly made cement with one of my dancing slippers. He said he was going to set it in the garden wall opposite the Poet's Nook. I suppose it was a lover's foolish idea."

"That wasn't foolish," Nancy replied. "It was one of the most sensible things Walter Heath ever did. That footprint clue in the crumbling wall will prove your claim to the Heath fortune against an impostor!"

Suddenly Nancy felt the woman beside her slump forward. In an instant the girl had caught her and placed her on the floor.

"Florianna has fainted," she called to Lieutenant Masters, who had walked down the corridor. "Please bring your flashlight."

Nancy was fearful the attack might be something worse than a faint, for the former dancer's pulse was very weak. When the light was flashed on her face, they saw it was chalk-white.

"The poor woman!" Nancy murmured. "She has been through so much!"

The policewoman berated herself for having left her first-aid kit in the car. She and Nancy worked over the still form, but Florianna did not revive.

"We *must* get her out of here!" said Nancy.

"I'll fire some shots," the lieutenant decided. "Will you stand by the window again, Nancy?"

Once more the officer climbed to the girl's shoulders. At this moment Florianna groaned.

"Wait!" cried Nancy. "If she's coming to, the shots will frighten her!"

The officer agreed and was glad Nancy had stopped her. As the victim on the floor regained consciousness, they could hear sounds of creaking boards at a distance.

"Listen!" commanded the policewoman.

Voices and footsteps could be heard echoing through the old castle. The lieutenant blew her police whistle.

"Where are you?" called a voice.

The officer shouted that they were below the trap door in the tower. Repeated blasts from the whistle and continuous knocking on the door guided the searchers. In another five minutes the three prisoners were released.

"Who is this?" asked one of the policemen, looking at the crippled Florianna.

The woman herself replied to his question. When Nancy

suggested she ought not to expend her strength talking, the woman insisted she felt much better.

"Who locked you in there?" the policeman demanded angrily.

"I'm not sure," Nancy answered. "Probably Mr. Hector Keep. He must have escaped."

"Oh, no he didn't," said a voice triumphantly. "We nabbed him climbing over a wall. Also these two birds."

Two more officers appeared. With them, handcuffed, were Cobb and Biggs. Behind the men was Hector Keep.

"This is an outrage!" the lawyer snapped. "You can't arrest me. I have a perfect right to be on this property. The others are trespassers."

Coolly, Nancy presented her evidence against Keep. She accused him of stealing jewellery from the estate, a claim that could be proved by photographs found in Walter Heath's box.

"And that is not the worst!" she said to him. "You pretended to look for the woman who was to inherit the estate, but you didn't try to find her because you knew she would expose your dishonesty. To protect yourself, you produced an impostor with whom you had made a bargain. When you found out I was on the trail of the real Florianna, you had her spirited away and locked in a dungeon here!"

"Ridiculous!" cried Keep furiously. "Lies—lies! Nothing but lies!"

The crooked lawyer had not yet seen Florianna, who was seated on the winding stairs in the tower. Playing her trump card, Nancy now stepped aside. Speechless, Keep stared at the crippled dancer.

"So what?" he demanded after a moment. "I had nothing to do with bringing her here! And she can't prove she's the missing dancer. Just look at her!"

"Oh yes, I can prove it!" Florianna retorted with spirit. "The imprint of my dancing shoe is embedded in a wall at Heath Castle. Furthermore, I still have the slipper that made the imprint!"

"What's that got to do with it? The real Florianna is at

the Riverview Hotel!" Keep blustered. "She has a note to prove her identity. A note signed 'Walt'."

"Don't you mean half a note?" Nancy inquired significantly. "I have the rest."

Cobb and Biggs looked startled. "You?" cried the latter. "Where did you find it?"

"At the factory after the explosion."

The men hung their heads guiltily, admitting they had been there. Biggs added:

"Hooker here found the note in a desk Mr. Keep sold. He tore it in two pieces, expecting the old man to cough up more money for the second half."

Nancy was startled to hear Cobb addressed as Hooker, though it confirmed what the girl had thought. To her inquiry if he were Jeddy's father, the man nodded sullenly that he was.

"Then that explains why the boy came to Heath Castle!" she exclaimed. "He learned about the estate from Joan. You in turn heard from your son that Florianna was missing, so you and Biggs got together. Biggs suspected his former employer had hidden some valuable things in the estate walls and you two convinced Mr. Keep he ought to hire you to look for them. When you men found them, you kept the things for yourselves."

"You guessed right, but I don't know how," said Biggs.

"I know nothing about any of this!" shouted the mortified lawyer.

"Mr. Keep, it looks as if the case against you is pretty serious," said Lieutenant Masters.

"I tell you I never saw these men before," Keep insisted. "Nor that crippled woman, either. Now all of you get out of here!"

For a second there was silence. Then slowly Florianna got to her feet. Her eyes ablaze, she pointed a finger at Keep, saying:

"Arrest that man! Arrest him for kidnapping!"

The wily lawyer's jaw dropped. Then he recovered himself. "The woman is crazy!" he shouted.

"The night you came to my farm and brought me here you wore a disguise," said Florianna accusingly. "At first I didn't recognize you. But your voice—I know your voice." The former dancer's eyes burned with hate as she added, "I shall prosecute you to the fullest extent of the law for Walter Heath's sake!"

Hector Keep knew he was beaten. There was too much evidence against him. But he would not give up the fight yet. Fairly hissing as he spoke, he looked straight at Nancy Drew and cried out:

"If you had minded your own business, there wouldn't have been all this trouble! But you needn't feel set up over it. You think there are treasures and money for Florianna. You're wrong. There's nothing in the estate. Not one penny!"

Chapter XXV

HEATH CASTLE RESTORED

THE dramatic scene in the tower of Heath Castle ended abruptly. The policemen and their prisoners went one way; Nancy, Lieutenant Masters, and Florianna headed for the Fenimore cottage.

When they reached her sister's home, Florianna asked Nancy to go in first and break the news, telling briefly of her present condition and of what had transpired during the past few hours.

"Oh, you've found my sister!" Mrs. Fenimore cried, after Nancy had spoken to her. "You wonderful girl! I don't care if we never have Heath Castle. To think Flossie is alive, and we can be together again!"

Gently Nancy warned her about Florianna's lameness. The news was a shock, but Mrs. Fenimore took it bravely, and hurried outside to greet her sister and help her into the house. Over and over the joyful women expressed their gratitude to the Drew girl.

Nancy said she was glad to have accomplished what she had, but could not be satisfied with leaving the case at this point. For days afterward the girl was tormented by all the distressing angles of the affair.

In the meantime Florianna had requested that all legal matters be attended to by Mr. Drew. The lawyer had lost no time in having Keep and the other men prosecuted, but his report to Nancy after an investigation was discouraging.

"Cobb and Biggs admit having found several bottles of valuable dye hidden in the cloister walls, as you suspected. But they sold them and kept the money. Since then they've spent it."

Nancy had been hopeful that Keep's dire prediction regarding the estate money would not be borne out, but such was not the case. Mr. Drew had discovered that the total Heath assets were twenty dollars and a ruined castle with a few pieces of furniture.

Account books showed huge sums had been paid to various detective agencies, supposedly for the purpose of conducting a search for the missing Florianna. This was not true. The wily lawyer had stolen the money instead.

"Unfortunately, we can't recover it," Mr. Drew remarked to his daughter. "It's all spent, and Keep has little of his own."

"How about the Heath pearl, Dad? You didn't find it?"

"No. I'll keep on trying, of course. Frankly, I don't feel hopeful about the prospect."

"The cloister walls may still contain a few treasures," the girl suggested, unwilling to admit total defeat.

"I've had the place searched, Nancy. Workmen even removed the Cinderella block of cement below the wall fountain, but there was nothing behind it. Everything's gone."

"Then what's to be done?" Nancy asked unhappily.

"Heath Castle will have to be sold for what it will bring, but I'm afraid that won't be much, considering its location and present condition. Florianna wants to keep the property, but she can't. She has barely enough funds to operate Clover Farm."

It was some consolation to Nancy that she had brought the sisters together, but she felt as if she had failed in one of the most vital tasks of her life.

"What if I did solve the mystery of Heath Castle?" she sighed. "I wasn't able to save the estate or help the Fenimores financially. And they need help so badly."

Nancy pondered the problem, but it was not until the next day that an idea came to her.

"I'll do it at once!" she declared. "Why didn't I think if it before?"

Dashing from the house, she got out her roadster and headed it for Mehearty's yacht home. The old man had barely greeted her when she excitedly propounded her scheme. Mehearty shook his head.

"Your idea's good, me lass," he agreed. "The only trouble is there's nary a whelk with dye in it left in that cove near the factory. The one that stained your friend's dress must a' been the last one alive."

"Then you've investigated the inlet since we were there?" Nancy asked.

Mehearty nodded.

"How about the beach at Heath Castle? Did you find anything there?"

"I never really looked," replied the old sailor, his face lighting up with hope. "Got a few clams that day I was there and then the trouble started. I never went back."

"Then let's go there right away and look!"

This time the girl rented a fast motorboat at Campbell's Landing and in a short while Mehearty was untying his little rowboat from it, and the two eager passengers were skimming across the water to the beach along the Heath estate.

"Lots of holes in the sand," said Nancy. "Do you suppose——"

The old clam digger set to work with a will. As Nancy watched, he brought up shell after shell from beneath the wet surface.

"Whelks!" he exclaimed excitedly. "And dye in 'em, too!"

Nancy wanted to dance for joy, but she controlled herself until Mehearty had dug up several dozen of the mollusks.

"You hit it, Miss Nancy!" he cried. "No doubt of it now," he grinned happily. "The place is full o' whelks."

Nancy felt as if a great weight had been lifted from her shoulders. Now Florianna would have an income. She could keep Heath Castle and fix it up.

"There's one more thing I must do," the girl thought as she and Mehearty returned to River Heights. "Talk to Cobb and Biggs."

Nancy drove directly to the jail and asked to speak first to Biggs. Since this was his initial offence, she decided he would be more likely to answer her questions truthfully than the former convict. She told the ex-chauffeur of her recent discovery and asked him if he had found any notations with the bottles of dye. When he demurred about answering, the girl suggested that his sentence might be lightened if he told her everything he knew.

"All right. I'll tell you," he said grudgingly. "I got nothing to lose."

The prisoner revealed that certain notes had been attached to each bottle of dye. Cobb Hooker had thought them of no value, but Biggs had hidden them under a certain flagstone in the cloister walk.

Nancy, overjoyed, hastened homeward to tell her father the good news. He looked at her fondly; and how proud he was of her!

"Nancy, my dear, you've saved the day for Florianna and the others," he said, smiling. Then he added, "I'll see what I can do for Biggs."

There were weeks of uncertainty before the dye project was put into effect. Mr. Drew advanced money to restore the button factory, part of which was to be used as a laboratory. Mehearty was placed in charge of beach operations and a young chemist, using the notations left by Walter Heath, gradually worked out several lovely colours from the dye found in the whelks.

During the waiting period, Nancy kept on wondering whether Walter Heath might not have made other discoveries. One idea which plagued her was why he had placed the Cinderella footprint in that particular spot. At last a solution came to her.

"The water in the fountain—it gave George and Bess and me a tremendous lift!" she thought excitedly. "Maybe it has special value!"

Again Nancy Drew had guessed correctly. An analysis of the water proved it to have unusually beneficial qualities, even curative effects in bone disorders. Arrangements were made with a bottling concern to market it.

Presently, with money pouring in from two sources, Florianna was given a free hand to establish the gardens at Heath Castle, just as they had been during her romance with its former owner.

The crippled woman moved to the estate, taking Mrs. Fenimore and Joan with her. For weeks she planned and supervised. Then came a wonderful day when she was able to fill the gardens with crippled children, now laughing and happy.

One afternoon, upon invitation, Nancy, Bess, George, Mr. Drew and Lieutenant Masters journeyed to the estate to view the many changes. The great gates stood open. The visitors drove up a winding road between avenues of trimmed hedge and trees. The three girls smiled when they recalled how different everything had seemed to them on their former visits there.

"It doesn't make me feel a bit creepy now," laughed Bess.

"Those burning eyes that watched me from behind the evergreen!" Nancy chuckled. "I know that they were Cobb Hooker's!"

"With him in jail, what's to become of Mrs. Hooker and Jeddy?" asked George.

"She's gone to work," replied the policewoman. "Jeddy has been sent to a special school, because only last week he was caught trying to snatch a purse. By the way, he was wearing his father's clothes."

"Just like the time when he ran off with my pocketbook and the pearl from old Mehearty's clam," Nancy said.

"It certainly was clever of you, Lieutenant Masters, to have solved that mystery and recovered the pearl for Nancy," said George.

The visitors got out of the car near the restored loggia and paused to admire the repairs which had been made to the crumbling walls. The gardens were a mass of bloom. The lawn in front of the castle was velvety smooth and free from weeds.

"How did Florianna ever accomplish so much in such a short time?" Nancy marvelled.

Several pigeons alighted near by. One of them, startled, flew to the parapet of the far tower of Heath Castle and began to coo. George smiled and whispered to Nancy:

"You were right. Those sounds we heard the first day we came here were only pigeons cooing!"

"I guess I let my imagination run away with me when I was locked in the tower," laughed Nancy. "At that time their cooing sounded human!"

Bess called the girls' attention to the children who had come out on the lawn to play. A few were in wheel chairs, but they pushed them about with amazing skill.

"Florianna is doing remarkable work with these youngsters," said Lieutenant Masters. "She's putting new spirit into them. Joan is developing into a fine little girl, too. She's proving to be a great help to her aunt."

"What is she doing?" asked Bess.

"Florianna is giving exercises to the children to restore nimbleness to their bodies. Joan does the demonstrating. And incidentally, Joan is the delight of her aunt. She's going to be a wonderful dancer some day."

"And take up where Florianna left off," said Bess dreamily.

The callers were greeted cordially by the mistress of Heath Castle and her sister, almost restored to perfect health and looking very attractive with a fashionable new coiffure. Tea was served on the terrace. Afterwards, Florianna invited her guests to the Poet's Nook, there to see the children who were lined up at the drinking fountain.

"The water is helping to build strong bodies," she said proudly. "Oh, it means so much to me to bring these boys and girls here! I'd never have forgiven myself if I had returned to a lonely life at Clover Farm."

Mr. Drew had been waiting for this very moment. Taking a tiny box from his pocket, he slipped it into Florianna's hand.

"A little surprise," he explained.

The woman slowly raised the lid. Nestled in purple velvet was a ring set with a huge pearl.

"Not the one Walt meant for me?" Florianna asked, dazed.

"Yes."

"But how did you recover it? I thought Hector Keep had found the ring and sold it."

"Dad was able to trace it," Nancy spoke up. "Mr. Keep failed to notice the inscription inside."

Tears filled Florianna's eyes as she read, " 'To my Cinderella.' I'll wear the ring always in memory of Walt," she whispered, her voice trembling. "Oh, Nancy, my dear friend, and Mr. Drew, you've made me very, very happy!"

Nancy smiled. She was glad the mystery had been brought to a successful close. Now she could devote more time to a new one on which she was working. Already Nancy was calling it *The Mystery of the Tolling Bell.*

Her gaze wandered along the stately cloister of Heath Castle. With the afternoon sun sinking low, the shadows in the passageway had never looked more beautiful.

"Don't thank me for helping you, Florianna," Nancy said earnestly, taking her hand. "Thank these crumbling walls. They provided the clue that brought you here. And forever they'll remain a symbol of mystery and romance!"